*ALSO PUBLISHED BY DIS VOIR*

PETER GRENAWAY

Series Historians

*The Historians Book 39: The Rise & Fall of Gestures Drama*

Series Fictions

*Gold*

*The Falls*

*Rosa*

*Fear of Drowning by numbers*

Series Script

*The Cook, the Thief, His Wife and Her Lover*

*The Pillow Book*

*Drowning by Numbers*

*The Belly of an Architect*

*Eight and a Half Women*

*The Baby of Mâcon*

*A Zed and Two Noughts*

*Nightwatching*

*Goltzius & the Pelican Company*

*The Food of Love*

*The OK Doll*

*Eisenstein in Guanajuato*

*Joseph*

*Lucca Mortis*

*Four Storms and Two Babies*

Series Art Book

*Papers*

# THE HISTORIANS
# BOOK 4

PETER GREENAWAY

THE HISTORIANS
BOOK 4

# TOYS

At the turn of the Millennium three historians attempted to make a fresh start at keeping a record of a rejuvenated world. They promised to write a full history of the years of the coming century. The first three historians were Lutumariner, Confumo and Parmitter. They were attempting to detail the new human population at its origin, to give this new community a start, to send them on their way, to record, however disputable and incomplete, their beginnings. To start with they needed a new population. They believed they needed if possible to make a record of the new conceptions. Once they had recorded their knowledge of post-war human conceptions in Book Zero, these three historians could go on to record the new Births in Book One, and Names in Book Two, and then perhaps Childhood Diseases in Book Three and then perhaps Toys in Book Four.

In the last decade of the century there would be historians to compile Book Ninety-Six on Fatal Illnesses, Book Ninety-Seven would record Deaths, Book Ninety-Eight would record Funerals & Memorials, Book Ninety-Nine would record Last Wills & Testaments and Book One Hundred would record Ghosts.

Here is Book Four to record Toys.

Three orphans of the last decades of war come together to describe toys emanating from the detritus of chaos, to uncover post-war conspiracies and mysteries and calumnies, post-war myths and lies, and post-war disgraces and excesses, to build a catalogue of toys out of the military disorder and pessimism where children's universal optimism for invention find meaning, entertainment and amusement. This text describes the making of some thousand toys that these orphans and their associates

 **variously discover, re-discover, invent and re-invent, and hopefully imagine will end up as a fulsome descriptive catalogue and maybe a public exhibition, and a comment on the recent wars, always remembering indeed the ironic fact that there is really no such thing as History, there can only be Historians.**

**The account begins like this:**

CATEGORY 1. WITH WAR ENDING IN UNSATISFACTORY CHAOS.

**Here are fifteen toys once owned by the ten-year old ginger-headed boy Eerio Padebourne. He often collected relics of the war. He was not alone in doing this, but he was probably the most persistent and the most methodical.**

*1. A white rag that had often been washed in a stream. It was knotted at one corner to make it easy to be tied to a stick to be made into a flag of truce in a structured playground exercise of battles. Now it was a toy but it obviously referenced much else.*

*2. A curved stick for trying to throw in circles in the hope that it would make a whizzing sound and return to the sender. Weapons were always in short supply. Returnable weapons had always been valuable.*

*3. A puddle-beater for making a smack on water, sometimes also used to hit small stones a great distance, certainly further than you could throw them unaided. It had been much appreciated in water-fights. "I kept my puddle-beater because it once belonged to my brother who was made blind from an enemy explosion."*

*We are often sentimental about toys. We often keep toys out of a sense of nostalgia.*

*4. A coalie that had once belonged to Brightly Presender's father who had been a soldier. If you looked through it, you could see how the world looked at night, an important aid in times of nocturnal attacks. Brightly Presender said that sometimes you could even see the sea with this coalie on the nights of a full moon. He seldom permitted people to use his coalie so that it was difficult to know if he was telling the truth. Now it was a harmless toy but it obviously referenced so much else. Eerio Padebourne often cradled it. On clear nights he sat with it on his lap whilst he looked at the stars. He had some idea that it would assist him on long journeys. Eerio Padebourne had been told that his father had died at night. Eerio Padebourne believed that his father had gone South on a moonless night, and that he had been carrying a coalie. Eerio stayed out at night perhaps with the coalie on his lap to hope to use it to see his father. All the time he thought of his father, he scratched at the tattoo on the inside of his lower left arm which had been placed there when he was a one-year-old baby. Most people had a war tattoo. It was customary.*

*5. Two wooden wheels on a wooden spindle fixed to a stick-handle. The left-hand wheel was worn considerably on its right-hand side so that the toy ran down slopes with a leaning to the left-hand side. Eerio Padebourne recognised it as a toy, though he was not so sure what it might have been originally. Perhaps some sort of chariot? There were rumours that its origins lay somewhere in the Wouverain Mountains. And with women. No matter. It was now a toy because Eerio Padebourne said it was a toy. He played with it, running it down slopes. He felt a certain identity with it. He often felt that his life would be lived with a leaning to the left-hand side. He ran with his two wooden wheels on a wooden spindle hoping for some affinity.*

*6. A broken whatcheater used for dangling down drains. You could never be certain what you might come up with. It had once been painted green, now it was painted purple.*

> *"Purple and green,*
> *And all colours in between."*

*Eerio Padebourne claimed that it was an item that could perhaps foretell things that might happen in the future, though it has to be said he had no great belief in such an idea.*

[10] **In just these six toys so much of the future was heralded. The white flag was an acceptance that peace was absolutely necessary. The curved toy suggested that all weapons should be handed in to the relevant authorities The puddle-beater was a remembrance that nostalgia was perfectly acceptable. The coalie was suggestive of the close necessary examination of the Future. The wheels, whichever way they leaned, left or right, was an unforeseen prophecy of the transport, real and metaphorical, of the eventual supremacy of the systems of the Wouverain Mountains. And the watcheater was an encouragement to see whatever was hidden, an important nod towards the efficacy of poetry, and a warning that, though at the present moment, the Future, not guaranteeable, was well worth our every optimism.**

**Eerio Padebourne was an orphan in the Wouverain Orphanage. He had Cubicle Nineteen in Ward Twenty-Three in the West Wing. When he lay in bed and looked out his own personal window he could see the Wouverain Mountain Foothills perhaps some twenty miles to the North across the Wouverain Plain. Beside his bed he had a glass-fronted cupboard where he kept his nightshirt, toothbrush and spare underwear, a second pair of boots, a magnifying glass, three exercise books with blue covers, copies of The Treatises of PastonCumber, Histories of The Thirty Years War, and various maps of the South, and the toys he had so far collected.**

*7. A man's leather boot stuffed with dried heather to make a nest for two speckled ceramic eggs that had been copied from the example of real eggs that had once been owned by a boy called Irony Fitness, who was an orphan and knew everything there was to be known about birds. And eggs.*

*8. A petrified fruit belonging to Tomity Ersweet. Perhaps it was a petrified apple. It had teeth-marks that had been made by Tomity's father's elder brother, who had died in a bloody skirmish on the Apro River. It was an object that referred to family relationships. It had been found in a tin box in a cave. Tomity had played with it when he was a child, fingering the teeth-marks with wonder. Eerio Padebourne knew it was likely that it had no uses in an adult world, but it could certainly be considered useful as a toy even as it sat in a dish on a sideboard. A toy to contemplate and wonder at its experiences.*

*9. A small, cork-stoppered pot of dried yellow black-eyed peas for making the sound, when shaken vigorously, of rain on a hot day. It certainly was not of course of itself, a rainstorm and it could not make you wet but it certainly encouraged you to remember rain on a hot day. It could be described as a symbolic thirst-quencher. More men died of thirst in the deserts of the South than were ever slain with arrows, slingshot, musket-balls or any other missile perfected by humans.*

*10. A carpet-beater that was sometimes used as a bat. It had been burnt from being flung on a fire in anger. The carpet beater had been used to beat carpets, that is what it was designed to do, and it had been used as a bat to hit a ball or a shuttlecock. So it had had two functions, to beat carpets and hit sporting missiles. The first deliberate and the second out of happenstance. And someone had certainly thrown it on a fire. It had a history. It was to be valued as an object. The best definition of it now was to consider it as a toy. As a toy it could become legitimate and be preserved and cherished. If it did not become a toy, no doubt it would be thrown away. It would end up in a kitchen midden or a rubbish heap. It was said that the reason it had been thrown on a fire was over a dispute between twins about whether or not there was indeed a sea in the world. This was an important question because the sea for many was becoming everyone's idea of a last resting place. A sea was becoming identified with a Heaven. But like a Heaven, no-one really believed in it, although most people very much wanted to.*

*11. Five red spots. They were applicable to any part of your body you wanted to make look ill, diseased or otherwse unsatisfactory. As a toy these five red spots offered much that satisfied a desire. To escape responsibilities. To dodge engagements. To be interestingly infectious. To gain preference in the matter of laying in bed until midday.*

*12. A frog skull. It had been painted with numbers and given a small, crimson, silk, forked tongue. It had a hinged jaw held to its upper cranium with black cotton thread. It was a sort of in-memoriam item. It reminded you of live things that were now dead. It reminded you of things that we could attempt to resurrect as something else.*

*13. A string for swallowing a knot and bringing it up again to sniff and smell the contents of your stomach. It was important to try to know what your insides could be like. It was dark in your interior. There were no lights in your interior to see anything with clarity.*

*14. A pointed flint kept in a draw-string purse. It could possibly be considered to be an ancient arrowhead, though you would have to have considerable amounts of imagination to believe such a thing. Eerio Padebourne, the ginger-haired boy, had such an imagination. And plenty of it. He was considered old for his age. And his experiences could well corroborate this fact. He was still only ten years old but he had experienced much. "I kept it because I have never seen another and thought it was rare, even unique."*

*15. A bordinlocker for seeing over fences if you were on the short side. Eerio Padebourne was perhaps considered short for his age. Members of the enemy had invariably been taller than he was. His sister, who was also on the short side, had made a doll that she cherished. It was two sticks taken out of the forest and tied crosswise together with butcher's string. Then she had stuck a crab-apple at the end of one of the sticks for a head and had broken the orange skin of the crab-apple in two places to indicate the eyes. She had entirely rejected the wax doll dressed in a white frilly skirt, given to her by her grandmother and much preferred the stick doll of her own making. This sort of activity was commonplace among children orphaned by the wars. Indeed it was commonplace among all children at all times. They would invariably treasure those toys invented by their own hands. They could be invested with all sorts of characteristics that were personal. Eerio Padebourne's sister, for example, shortened the stick that represented the height of her body because she herself was on the short size and needed to identify with her self-fashioned doll. It was impossible to shorten the height of her grandmother's doll. That would have been both an impertinence towards her grandmother who she revered, and would have been iconoclastic because it would have been an act of violence. This sort of thinking was characteristic of so many of the toys that found their way into Eerio Padebourne's toy collection.*

*A well-fashioned pre-war cart and horse toy was rejected and replaced with a wooden brick from the parquet flooring of an old house. This wooden brick could be a cart and horse indeed but could also be a boat on a river, a gull in the sky, a mouse in a tunnel, a brother asleep in bed. The immense imaginative store of ideas in a child's memory and capacity to invent and to reconstruct and indeed to customize to fit with what was necessary to survive and thrive, was almost unlimited.*

## CATEGORY 2. WITH WAR ENDING IN UNLIMITED CHAOS.

**Here are twenty-three more toys once owned by the ten-year-old ginger-headed boy Eerio Padebourne. They were collected together after the first sixteen toys which were always considered to be the very heart of his collection. He kept these twenty-three toys in a locked chest of drawers in his ward's ante-room down one flight of stairs from where he slept.**

*16. A chain with a bar for your knees to prevent you from closing your legs. It was sometimes called a ginnie-drafty. It had come from a whorehouse. As a toy, it was used in games as a check on pretend horses who would not behave. "I kept it because it smelt ugly, and not at all because it had some sort of influence over horses."*

[14] *17. Three painted oak galls joined together "to represent the sun, the moon and the earth in collision." It had been owned by Silkie Cuss, a studious boy given most of his time to looking at the night sky. Silkie Cuss spent most of his days sleeping. Silkie Cuss was also an orphan of the Continental Wars. His painted oak galls gave him a symbolic place in the Universe. That, and the war tattoo on his lower left arm which had originally read "All is for the best except for the worst." But the tattoo had been inefficiently erased and now could be said to not say anything reliably decipherable.*

*18. A pig's bladder filled with Collie Highbrow's sister's farts obtained by using a funnel, a meal of mashed beans, and a great deal of blackmailing persuasion that had left her deeply distressed. Collie Highbrow and his sister were orphans of the wars. It was said that her father had been tortured by having straws pushed violently up his nose. They said that was why Collie Highbrow and his sister walked the world with their heads turned to the sky, as though trying to avoid an intense pain in their upper nostrils. Indeed, some went so far as to say that their surname was a reflection of that gesture of the head and the pain so endured. That cannot be because the slightest perusal of their family genealogies demonstrates the surname went back at least thirty generations which is considerably before the Continental Troubles began.*

*19. A barrow with a broken leg called The One Wheeled Crippled Racer. It was in the possession for a time of three sisters who lived near a disused mine. They had a memory of rails for transporting things. For a time Eerio Padebourne kept it alongside Item Five, which was described as "Two wooden wheels on a wooden spindle fixed to a stick-handle." He could see that there might very well be a connection. He could imagine that these two objects, Toy Five and Toy Nineteen, would sit well together when they were exhibited. They might even share a label.*

*20. A Pollyhooker. Used sparingly for lifting up girls' skirts. It had been confiscated several times by conservative teachers and angry parents with vulnerable daughters.*

*21. A cow thighbone riddled with the holes of a saw-weevil. Most of the holes were filled with dried snot by two boys in bed with an incurable lung disease, sometimes called the Foggy Dew on account of the drips of lemon-coloured liquid that formed on the end of the nose and were reminiscent of October dewdrops in a hawthorn hedge.*

*22. A yardbittery knobknoberry, meaning an object of fascination. Its purpose and origin was not completely known. It could be used as an offensive weapon. And often was. It was certainly an object expressing authority. A child owning a yardbittery knobknoberry could legitimately claim to become a leader of some sort. One particular owner said, "Looking to wield some idea of authority, I kept it."*

*23. Dried-out Sucksauce in a paper boat. A delicacy from before the Continental Wars. It was worth remembering as a reminder of a Golden Age, even if that Golden Age had been calamitous and scarcely deserved a reputation for being golden. Such is often the reputation of Golden Ages.*

*24. A humper. There was much ambiguity about this item, its title could suggest so many things. Some regarded this very characteristic as an advantage, most did not. To be many things weakly, they argued, was confusing; to be adamantly one thing only was comforting. To be "adamant" was to be exceedingly determined. The noun associated with the word adamant is adamance, to rhyme with romance. But this noun is rarely encountered anymore. It is considered to be archaic. We could say that the word is generally out of use.*

*25. A bat made from willow wood, with a handle bound around with cat-gut secured with fish glue. It was now a peaceful toy, but it was possibly modeled on a shortened halberd which was anything but peaceful.*

*26. A single wheel painted with spots that became circles when the wheel was spun fast. "A sure indication that speed is a change-maker," said Phistrone, who only had one leg.*

[16] *27. A miniature bow and three miniature arrows flighted with brown chicken feathers. It was a scaled-down version of an adult object and was now considered legitimate as a toy.*

*28. A small book with an incomprehensible hand-written text and several burnt pages, used to impress small children who could not read who were threatened to be set alight if they did not pay sufficient attention to their elders and betters.*

*29. A battered metal dish for porridge whose rim repeatedly had been stamped with a trefoil dye. If you settled it at the right angle, the dish ran down hills well and was desirable.*

*30. A tarnished military badge which had a disfigured design, which could have featured, if you looked at it from one angle, like a lion fighting a snake, or, if you looked at it from another angle, like an old man with long hair smoking a long-stemmed pipe."I enjoyed its ambiguity, so I kept it, though some may say I was foolish to keep something that showed I was nostalgic for the wars."*

*31. A hook used for dragging, dredging and delving in shallow streams like the Nadder, the Firmly, the Gedda Brook, the Sledge, the Marrow, the Brount, the Borrow and the Blade, all of which feature in the post-war Shallow Rivers Guide.*
*Such a hook had a reputation for dredging up corpses and was used with reluctance for that reason.*

*32. A hat with a small and dirty feather in its hat-band that was judged originally to have been blue, perhaps it came from a kingfisher's wing. Matterly Smalls used the hat as a bag for carrying berries, often blue-berries. His sister used it for collecting spent musket balls that she had found on the known and recognised war-fields. Sometimes spent musket balls were blueish in colour. Perhaps this was evidence of being associated with hot gunpowder. Matterly Smalls and his sister were orphans from the war. They had been repeatedly, shamefully and balefully exploited. They had partially erased tattoos that identified them as being late-war babies. "Tattoos" because it had been a military practice for children to have tattoos and "late" because the practice had been condemned and attempting to erase shameful tattoos had become common.*

*33. A broken cup for putting mud in. "Cups like this were manufactured, I was told, in the deep South. They were items of privilege. For a child to put mud in a vessel like this was insulting that privilege."*

*34. Another yardbittery knobknoberry, this time made of tin. Tin had a strange reputation. It was often considered cheap. Perhaps this was because toys were often made of tin. And toys were not considered to be very valuable. Children's toy soldiers were often made of tin. There is a children's story to suggest this very characteristic written by an author who frequently recorded the number of times he was sick, which was twice every week and three times on Sundays. The tin soldier in this story, one of twenty-five such soldiers, only had one leg because the tin spoon melted down to manufacture the soldiers had become exhausted.*

*35. A bag for carrying sling stones. "It had a cord for your shoulder that used to be threaded in my mother's blouse, the dark red one she used to wear on Friday evenings when the men had money to spare and would pay her to undress at the fair to hang their wedding rings on her nipples. My mother had very sticky-out nipples. Like school-hat pegs, she said. She said it was because she had breast-fed me until I was four years old, and I had fearsome gums and teeth. My mother had never owned a wedding ring."*

*36. A marked-up wooden block on a frayed cord, once used for throwing at a midget at a traveling fair to score points to win a toady-bowl. Both during the wars and certainly afterward, short people had great trouble finding employment and suffered much humiliation in order to survive.*

*37. A small metal scriber for scratching your name on tree-trunks, furniture and desks. It once belonged to Hardy Spits who used it to scratch Palley's eye out. Palley was the deerhound bitch that bit Hardy Spits when he drowned her puppies. This small metal scriber could also be useful for Historians to write history. To write down indeed descriptions of toys which in their various ways represented what was happening in the world in the aftermath of war, represented much implicit violence, much cruelty, much misogyny, much attention to undesirable sex and its depredations and, it has to be admitted, its regretful heady excitements. Perhaps for some people, the word "regretful" is unnecessary.*

*For a long time after the Continental Wars could be said to have truly finished, there lingered still much bullying, a continuing sense of competition, and a long stale taste in everyone's mouth. However perhaps for some people the wars were addictive.*

*38. Parmitter described a toy he found in the street. "A dove's wing that was pretty grubby from being over-stroked. This had become a toy that reminded you of Nature's desirability and its unintended despoilation," said Parmitter.*

CATEGORY 3. WAR ENDING IN ATTEMPTS TO FIND PEACE.

## Some toys which the boy Eerio Padebourne did not own, but wished he did.

*1. A miniature steeple aspiring to touch the sky. Made of wood. Steeples were often made of wood since wood was so amenable to changing stresses and strains, was comparably pliable and was comparatively easy to fashion and manipulate.*

*2. A small boat made of wood soaked in wax to help it float. "The wax may have been part of a ceremonial candle at some time in its history. You could smell privilege."*

*3. A small coin-machine made of wood, for keeping your copper farthings safe from thieves.*

*4. A wind-up sister. Was it a sister? Or was it just a doll? Dolls were a problem.*

*5. A monkey from the South.*

*6. A grand cuscorn hat.*

*7. A musical instrument to awaken ghosts. It was shaped like a cow horn and came wrapped in a yellow flag made from a petticoat.*

*8. A sliver of mirror for seeing your own smile, and also for looking at your anus from between your legs."How many people in the world have not seen their anuses through their legs because they had never owned a sliver of mirror?"*

CATEGORY 4. WAR ENDING IN HOPEFUL EXPECTATION.

**Three toys which the ten-year-old ginger-haired boy Eerio Padebourne thought he still owned, but was not able to locate anymore.**

*1. A gadget somewhere for bringing fierce horses into his life. It could have had sharp points in its making but Eerio believed the horse would never have been harmed.*

*2. Perhaps a block of glass. Now almost lost. You could see what you wanted to see in it.*

*3. A painted picture of his mother where he thought he remembered the eyes moving when you tipped it sideways. Pictures can be good substitutes for the real thing. At least for a while, until the truth kicks in.*

[20] CATEGORY 5. WAR ENDING IN UNSATISFIED DESIRE.

**One toy which the ginger-haired boy Eerio Padebourne stole from a girl who he found standing on her hands in wet grass at the bottom of the Wouverain Orphanage Garden. Just by the broken fence and the non-flowering cherry tree. The girl's name was Esquila Fontenay.**

*1. A jill-in-a-box that laughed like a queen when you opened the lid.*

CATEGORY 6. WAR ENDING IN UNSATISFIED BUSINESS.

**Fourteen toys which the boy Eerio Padebourne had seen that were owned by other children.**

*1. A top-heavy crimson thing that span.*

*2. A collection of twenty-two dolls all dressed in black that represented the family of an executioner - a mother, a step-mother, a father, a step-father, an aunt, a step-aunt, a grandmother, a step-grandmother, a grandfather, a step-grandfather, a nephew, a step-nephew, a niece, a step-niece, an uncle, a step-uncle, a cousin, a step-cousin, a sister, a step-sister, a brother and a step-brother.*

*3. A thing on six metal legs that, when wound up, could sometimes climb a vertical brick wall if there was no wind about.*

*4. A set of five fishing floats in a tin with a lid. One with a torn red butterfly lure. One with a burnt jay's feather. One with an imitation minnow made of painted wood that had been in water so often that all of its colour had been washed away. One that looked like a green caterpillar, squashed at the head-end which might, as likely as not, be on account of a fisherman holding it in his teeth whilst he fixed the bait on the hook. One that had a swiveling metal bit called a 'minuette', save it did not swivel anymore on account of rust.*

*5. A satchel with compartments for seeds that Emile Froughter had filled with stolen glass drops from the hanging lamps in the Convention House at Ripple.*

*6. A cockscomb for day-luck, and a set of crow's feet for night-luck.*

**The historian Lutumariner said that a toy could be something that is a non-functioning replica of something else, something not to be taken too seriously, something small or miniature. The Historian Confumo might take exception to some of those definitions. He might quarrel with the words "non-functioning", "replica", "not to be taken too seriously", "small" and "miniature". His greatest agreement might be the phrase "a non-functioning replica of something else". However he would find the word "non-functioning" problematic. He might simply prefer to say, "a replica of something else". And that something else conventionally, very often existed in the world of adults.**

*7.A block of wood painted orange set in the middle with an iron ring. It was once used as a doorstop in a stable.*

*8.An almost see-through strip of birch bark to be held across the eyes to pretend to see the sun at the time of an eclipse, if there was one.*

*9.A faded painted signpost saying Pass-Through-Street with a finger pointing.*

*10. A chewed half-brick from a barn where a wolfhound had once given birth to seven whelps. Such a large brood was unusual.*

[22] *11. A paper mache model of a mountain with white painted snow on the top. The full moon was attached to the mountains with a stiff wire. It was once said that the dark patches on the moon were seas. The astronomer with the mole on his cheek who was arrested for publishing such an idea, had said as much, and this was considered a dangerous thing to say because it set up expectations of the idea of seas on earth. Many people grew to believe that the moon was delivered from the earth much like a child is born from a woman. You can imagine what fantasies were started up by such an idea, commencing with considerations of the amniotic fluid and activities like the "breaking of the waters. "People brought umbrellas in expectation of being rained upon by the moon."*

*12. A doll stuffed with smelly trimmings from the tannery.*

*13. A face that was said to look like The Compounder indistinctly chalked onto a piece of slate. "It was said to be pretty old. If you dared to attempt to rub it out with a wet rag or the spittle-wetted cuff of your sleeve, or a lady's handkerchief, you, like it, would become indistinct. Indeed, it was said, you would as good as disappear like it had almost disappeared. Morper peed on it, and although he did not disappear, his willie did, and he became a girl. This last statement was not really believed, but it had a sort of sensational ring to it that made it repeatable as a story." Besides,"Tidimouse" Morper was somewhat ambiguous in his sexuality. For example he sometimes sat down to piddle.*

*14. A bar of pig-fat white soap molded to look like two lips kissing each other. It was popular and very familiar and made in a wooden mold and sold cheaply. It was given traditionally on birthdays to children but had a smell of lavender and was often coveted by adults. Many people had washed with such soap. And when they washed the intimate parts of their bodies with this soap, they ostentatiously smacked their lips in a kissing motion.*

Many toys have a substance that does not require them to be a replica of anything. And the Historian Parmitter would argue that all toys are functioning. He would also demonstrate that all toys are not necessarily to be played with, nor are they insignificant trifles, nor should they always not be taken seriously, and are not necessarily by definition small or miniature. He would certainly have said that toys harbored in replica a representation of everything that there was in the world. You can easily see here how meaning is allusive, making the practice of History a dubious vehicle for Truth. Even that word "allusive" is allusive; it can often be confused with the words "elusive" and "illusive".

The Historian Lutumariner said that he would like to meet the orphan Eerio Padebourne. He said that they might have affinities. Most people were not so sure what "affinities" might mean.

CATEGORY 7. SOME BELIEF IN THE BENEFITS OF PEACE.

> *1. A rag that may have been at one time a hat. It was found abandoned on a nursery floor at Gopping; it still smelled faintly of milked-stained porridge oats sweetened with wild honey.*

The orphan Eerio Padebourne included in his collection of toys, five items that balanced on the edge of being, and not being, toys. When is a toy not a toy? Are these following five items in fact toys? They were used obsessively by very small children who invested great store by them, and who fell into great distress when the coveted item was lost or stolen or removed from their sight or touch. Their confidence and sense of security was often related to this precious item which in essence was a sheet or a blanket or an item of clothing or even just a rag relied upon to be a comfort.

Are toys created to be a comfort? The answer must surely be yes.

[24] *1. A white cotton rag that had been patched frequently with pieces taken from a faded yellow chemise complete with cloth buttons. The whole had been dipped in a pale blue dye that had turned the yellow patches green. One edge of the white cotton-rag had been turned back and hemmed. This was the edge that gave a handle on the cloth permitting it to be dragged along the ground. The cloth was grubby and grew grubbier the further from the hemmed edge, ending in straggling threads that were entirely black from being dragged through damp soot. Its hiding place had been a chimney. Many people hid what they considered to be valuable or immodest or indiscreet in a chimney. Jewels, love-letters, severed heads, money, weapons, hearts, dead babies. Maybe they thought the fire lit below in the hearth would save and protect them. And few people are going to be pleased to be rummaging about in sooty, dirty chimneys. That way the enemy missed finding the severed head of the military dictator which had been decapitated after death, and then the bastard baby son of Porley Stratford, and then the Fastcliff Rubies, and then the beloved blistered tortoise of the small man Laudie, and finally, Caterwaul's underlinen as evidence of some ill-understood misbehaviour.*

*2. A linen-cloth rag sewn with the representation of red lions. The three-year old owner of this treasure believed the lions to be cats. He sometimes pointed at them and meowed. The original linen cloth may have been a privy-room curtain because some sniffers really believed it still smelt of excrement, for it was well known that in lieu of finding any other suitable material, those taken short sometimes wiped their fingers on the privy-curtains. Before possibly being a privy-curtain, this fragment of linen-cloth could have been an underskirt. The present three-year old owner's name was Articular, Artie, for short. He was an orphan. Many orphans thought that being an orphan without parents was the regular state of things. Who or what indeed were parents?*

**There was indeed a considerable amount of hiding and concealment going on, so much so that many people were making inquiries. "What are you hiding, Esquerelle, that I might be interested in?" The reply was almost always inevitably, "Nothing". It became a sort of society game, played with a wry smile, but it masked a real insecurity. It even began to infect the potential exhibition of toys that was currently being put together by the ten-year-old ginger-headed boy Eerio Padebourne.**

**Eerio thought often of how best to exhibit these particular items. He wanted to display each of the items in Category 7 as a single entity. Should they be displayed conventionally on white-painted shelves?**

> *3.A grey woolen rag that was patched with red linen patches and was marked with a little blood. There was no knowing its original purpose. On first examination, all the red patches were considered to be indeed linen patches. It was only later that some of the red colour was discovered to be blood. It was wondered whether or not, if this was an act of concealment, it was disguising violence of some kind.*

> *4. A rag that was as long as a banner-flag and still bore rusty marks that could have come from the nails that had fixed it to a flag-pole. Perhaps related to this possible usage, the item should be displayed as a flag or a banner. And perhaps it should be displayed in the open air so that winds or breezes should give it motion. A flag or banner is particularly designed for motion.*

> *5. A white cotton rag cut approximately in the shape of a child with a large head, short arms, and negligible legs. This rudimentary visual description of a child's idea of itself is not uncommon. The fascination for self starts importantly at the head and diminishes as you travel down the body. Perhaps very small children, apart from a desire for personal comfort, were not really very interested in such things.*

[26] **To date, the ten-year-old, ginger-headed boy Eerio Padebourne had collected items which he described as "toys" and had either owned, wished he had owned, thought he might have owned at one time or had seen in the possession of other children. He was eager to bring them all together in one place so that he could make an over-view.**

**He took what he could of them to his friend, the nine-year-old, blonde-haired boy Irium Bostero, who agreed to store them with his collection of sticks under the stairs in ward thirty-one of the Orphanage at Wouverain.**

**Most authorities eventually considered Eerio Padebourne's toys to be at the very centre of The Toy Collection when it was finally first exhibited much later in Wouverain City and then definitively exhibited and catalogued in PastonCumber, the capital associated with the Wouverain Mountains.**

**Eerio Padebourne reasoned that toys were important evidence of how the Continent had behaved in the last three decades, and should be treasured. Historians should respect toys. The bearded Historian Lutumariner, sucking at his white whiskers, agreed with him.**

# STICKS

CATEGORY 8. THE START OF POST-WAR APATHY BECAUSE HOPE IS ALWAYS LIMITED.

**Irium Bostero had a collection of sticks that he kept under the Big Stairs in the Orphanage at Wouverain.**

> *1. A Prime Stick. "Sticking is an aimless, or predominantly aimless activity with a stick, mainly involving activities of swishing, that is to say making side to side movements in the free air to make a swishing noise, making prodding and poking movements down holes, or among the roots of trees, or in*

*swishing, that is to say making side to side movements in the free air to make a swishing noise, making prodding and poking movements down holes, or among the roots of trees, or in puddles and ponds to make splashings of various kinds. Sometimes a stick is used to scuff up water to splash friends and sometimes enemies, or for banging on tree trunks and the backs of knees of friends and sometimes enemies, or for trailing on walls, tree-trunks, palings, fences and railings, if they can be found, or for dragging on soft ground to make trail marks in straight lines and in patterns, or for throwing in the air and sometimes, but not always, for throwing the stick vertically but seldom horizontally, sometimes with a twirling motion, or for striking at cats and other animals. A Prime Stick was kept indefinitely and could sometimes become a valuable heirloom, and could be handed on to grateful new owners."*

*2. A stick for pinging. A special activity for a stick involving the fixing of a clay lump to the springy end of the stick, and hurling the clay lump from off the stick with a from-over-your-shoulder motion.*

*3. A stick for pretending to be an old man, and fulfilling the riddle that ends, "... and what walks on three legs in the evening?"*

*4. A short thickish stick "... for the prodding of young girls to pretend that they are being fathered upon." This stick is gestured with a great deal but never ever used for the supposed intended purpose. It was a fantasy stick, hardly understood by anyone who had ever owned it. Once or twice it was held between the legs of a fat boy called Forester, but it was not clear that he knew what he was doing. Once it was sucked by a girl called Ostricka, but she was trying to change its intended pretend function to that of a stick of sweet licorice, because she was dumb, having been struck in the throat by an angry swan when she was three years old, and was now being obliged to mime everything. "But she was very good at miming, and we always understood her."*

*5. A stick of a pliant nature which could be bent into an arc and swept through autumn spider-webs to make a net on which to arrange flower petals in patterns.*

**CATEGORY 9. THE START OF THE POST-WAR FANTASIES IN THE WIDER WORLD WHERE CHILDREN COLLECTED TOYS.**

## Special category of sticks used as wands.

*1. A peeled willow stick with a naturally curving handle that had been whittled to show a woman's head with staring eyes.*

*2. A glass rod, broken at one end. It had served a kitchen purpose at some time.*

*3. A black stick with a forked handle said to have been the property of the orator Blackener who used it to wave at the crowds to make them disappear.*

*4. More a stave than a wand. It had a brass door-knob fitted at one end. It belonged to the orator Smutney who had racks of canes and sticks in the corridors of his house. He used this particular three metre-long stick to beat time on the wooden floor-boards in his metrical oratorical classes. One evening, ferociously banging his wand, he struck his foot and drew blood. He was not a very washed sort of man and the wound festered, became gangrenous and he died.*

*It has to be said that after he had died, the orator Smutney was not especially missed. The stave came into the possession of a small studious boy called Endon who might have been Smutney's nephew. Endon carved his name along the stick's long length, adding fictitious first names he might liked to have owned, like Eppiment, Cruel, Fowlness, Appropriator, Jacon, Fleece and Mortonberry. He did this to fill up the space. By thus personalizing the stave, the stave curiously lost its aura, and essentially it degenerated into a toy. Lutumariner would never have used the word 'degenerated' in such a context.*

# BALLS

**CATEGORY 10. THE START OF SOME POST-WAR COMPETITIVE BEHAVIOUR.**

**If Irium Botero collected sticks, then Jendro Hisloper, his eleven-year old, black-haired friend, collected balls.**

*1. A ball made from twine tightly bound around a white pebble taken from a stream bordering the Wouverain Mountains which were largely inhabited by women who certainly knew their own minds.*

*2. A ball made from sticky horse hair, taken mainly from a much-admired mare called Astute.*

*3. A ball of sweet suet.*

*4. A crumpled rag bound around by string, the whole soaked in sugar water. If you licked it, you could certainly taste the sugar. Aster Barian said, "I kept it because it was a sweet and vulnerable thing that gave me great pleasure to look at."*

*5. Fiancer's pinafore wrapped around tightly with its own strings.*

*6. A crock of pressed leaves cemented together with horse dung, "made to be kicked." said Falisse, "because you did not want to get horse-shit on your fingers".*

*7. A ball for rolling on water.*

*8. A ball for your body made of air trapped in a leather bag, that you can hold under your chin, under your arms or at the back of your crooked knee to relieve all manner of pressures and be a comforter.*

*9. A ball that bounces very high indeed. So high in fact that small children thought the ball might be able to see the sea.*

**On examining the first draft of the Toy Catalogue, as a proposal some years later to publishers, Parmitter said, that Category Eight and Category Nine on Irium Botero's sticks and Jendro Hisloper 's Category Ten on balls, could be said to represent respectively masculine and feminine principles. There is perhaps some irony involved in thinking of balls as feminine. Curiously Parmitter, always eager to make remarks of a sexual nature never drew attention to this fact. Perhaps he thought it too obvious.**

**Jendro Hisloper was aware that the space under the stairs in the Big Orphanage was not going to be large enough to house all the collected toys of himself, Eerio Padebourne and Irium Bostero.**

**Eerio Padebourne suggested asking the Wouverain Orphanage pastry-cook, Izek Bable, if they could use the empty scullery at the back of the kitchens in the Big Orphanage Building as a temporary storage-space. The pastry-cook, a retired soldier, had agreed.**

**Eerio Padebourne was eager to include in his collection of toys, those places and spaces where certain games involving balls, spinning-tops, dinner plates, saucers and other moving items could be played. He discussed this proposition with the pastry-cook, Izek Bable, who agreed enthusiastically. The difficulty in this proposition was how to make it viable. What would be the evidence and how could it be presented? It was agreed that certainly there should be a text description in a catalogue, associated with drawings and diagrams, and maps annotated with arrows. And the moveable physical objects involved should, if possible, be collected and displayed in a potential exhibition.**

# TOY-ASSOCIATED SPACES

## CATEGORY 11. WHILST CONSIDERING THE POST-WAR TERRITORIES.

**Jendron Hisloper marked on a map, large landscape features utilized to play ball-associated games. Jendron Hisloper, like the Historian Parmitter, was greatly interested in maps.**

*1. The game of Tymower. This game was habitually played on the long grassed slope at the Tymower Estate. Ten wooden balls fashioned out of oak and painted red and green to be run down a mile-long grass slope at the Tymower Estate which had been recently mowed to clean off the ragwort. Unevenness in the incline, patches of dock, mole-hills, cow-pats and sleeping cows were regarded as legitimate handicaps, hindrances and interruptions. Competitors were allowed to soak the balls overnight in water to increase their weight to help them roll faster.*

*2. The game of Dovey Water. This game was originally played on a stretch of slow-moving water with forty coloured wooden balls hollowed out to make them buoyant in water. The balls traditionally were associated with a bend in the river from a bridge to a weir on the Dovey Stream. Competitors dropped the coloured wooden balls through a rusting metal grid stolen from a windmill used to grind powders for making paint, into the sluggish stream from a pack-horse bridge. The first ball to strike the metal guard-rail of the weir four miles downstream was considered the winner. The river flowed so slowly, there was time for a drink and a conversation in the local hostel before walking to the winning post to check out who had won.*

*3. Upton Pages Rebounds. This game was initially played against a nearly vertical cliff of red sandstone. A dozen coloured rubber balls kept in a leather horse-feed bag hung on a hook on the back of the iron door at Upton Pages. Competitors threw the balls between a high and low marker on the wall whose uneven*

[32] *surface made a calculation of the rebound almost unknowable, thus wrong-footing the would-be catcher. The winner was declared according to a continuity of successful catches off rebounds. The scores were seldom very high.*

*4. The Ferryman Road Game. Played at an ancient dry-stone wall. Six wooden balls painted white so that they could be seen clearly at dusk. They were first brought into play at an ancient dry-stone wall that bounded the Ferryman Road outside Amerogen Superior. Irregular bounce patterns due to the uneven surface of the wall tested a competitor's judgment of catching a rebound. The local tenant-farmers objected to the game since, as like as not, repeated play dislodged the stones and let the sheep through to wander into the road and become ill from eating the henbane on the roadside verges locally called Cliches.*

*5. The game played at the facade of the abandoned Buttermark Town-Hall in Hearing CrossWays. A ball called the Smuck was thrown against the facade of the abandoned Buttermark Town-Hall, a century-old brick façade that had been due for demolition for some thirty years. The facade was some thirty feet high, with ledges and window-sills that acted as handicaps for the thrown bladderskin ball called the Smuck to bounce back to the thrower to be caught with one hand. A right-hand catch was awarded ten points, a left-hand catch doubled the score. The last person to touch a ball without catching it was always responsible for its retrieval. When girls played, the boys opened the seven windows to permit an opportunity for the Smuck to enter the building to be retrieved, thus providing an opportunity for the female player to be goosed in the dim light of the interior. Sometimes the game stopped for twenty minutes whilst a player used the opportunity of a lost ball to kiss and fumble an unwary female. Once the game stopped for half an hour when five boys found it necessary to search the second floor for a lost ball, and a young girl new to the district ran home without her skirt, and crying her eyes out. Four boys were later thrashed for moral turpitude. A fifth boy escaped punishment and used his experience when he grew up to become a pimp.*

**The female who had been seen standing on her hands in wet grass at the bottom of the Wouverain Garden near the non-flowering cherry-tree by Eerio Padebourne, was twelve years old. Her name was Esquila Fontenay. It was rumoured that her mother had died from swallowing three quarts of a Southern crab-apple ginger vinegar. Though no-one believed this story. This story was far too insignificant for the mother of the intrepid and adventurous female, Esquila Fontenay. Her mother's name may have been Perpetua. And it was distantly rumoured that she might have carnally known the Historian Lutumariner.**

**Esquila Fontenay came to the Wouverain Orphanage by way of an abusive father. Esquila Fontenay and Eerie Padebourne became confederates and then because of their enthusiasm for the Jill-in-a-Box that laughed like a queen when you opened the lid, they became friends. They agreed to take turns to borrow this delectable toy. To listen to the laughter was to be filled with great goodwill. They sat at night in a spinney on the side of the PasterPaley Hill in the Wouverain Mountains, opening and closing the box till its hinges fell off and the pastry cook, Izek Bable, used a cookery instrument to fix the join.**

*6. A game to be played in a water meadow. Balls made of rolled up twine were hurled back and forth across a meadow stream in an attempt to get the opposing team-members to fall into the water as they reached out to catch it, or, at the very least, to be splashed. The game was unplayable in winter, the stream being too wide from flooding or else it was invariably frozen over.*

*7. The Game of Pill. Played ideally in a sand dune. A steep sand dune near Arestoria was the initial location. The sand dune could be slid down on a birch-bark sledge, where the game-*

*players had to hold a heavy ball called The Pill without dropping it or letting it touch the sand. In March when the winds became very strong from the East, the sand was blown about and consequently rearranged, creating new ridges and hollows such that the previous year's experience of knowing the slope became almost irrelevant. Becoming expert at negotiating the sharp bends and deep turns of the long incline had to be relearnt.*

*8. A game played on a section of asphalted road on a hillside near the Panning Tree. It had a gutter on either side that was suitable to roll balls down at reasonable speeds. A competitor ran ahead of the rolling ball, sweeping away all possible impediments to its progress with a broom. The impediments might be leaves, twigs, small stones, even maybe a dead bird or a mouse corpse. Or even a live but sleepy toad.*

### CATEGORY 12. SETTLING UP THE POST-WAR TERRITORIES.

## Smaller landscape spaces associated with balls.

*1. A space between a large yellow stone and a brick wall marked with chalk crosses, where girls went to play Frog's Legs, a game involving leap-frogging with a ball.*

*2. A space in a field between a broken fence and a mulberry bush where solitary children learnt to juggle Lapidary Balls.*

*3.A large covered space considered by small children to be the six-sided coffin of an ogre where you could play Sevens without being observed.*

*4. A curved space at the edge of a wood considered to be shaped like one of those saucepans for stewing apples used frequently in the South. It had once been used for spooning because you could not be seen from the road. Now it was used for dribbling the Catchpoll.*

*5. A space in a wood thought of as a pot of figs that obliged small children to burp and larger children to fart. Sometimes the rituals were played with a ball. The pot of figs space, some said, had once been a display ground for garotting prisoners of war. Commentators said that before they died, terrified prisoners normally vomited, thus it was nicknamed the Sick Pit.*

*6. A space that was considered to be triangular, though strict geometry would not have agreed. It was also considered to be the entrance to the lair of a wounded bear. A game frequently played on the site by war-orphans was a loose variation of "Who's Afraid of Cannibals", whose title might very well originally have been "Who's Afraid of Cannon-Balls?"*

*7. A space under the wooden stairs in a stable for mules where small children went to wet the ball with their spittle to make it heavier in a game called "Strangers and Home People".*

CATEGORY 13. THE POST-WAR RESETTLEMENTS THAT NEEDED THINKING ABOUT.

**Eight smaller landscape spaces that the three boys, the black-haired Jendro Hisloper, the blonde-haired Irium Bostero and the ginger-haired Eerie Padebourne researched together. These eight landscape toy-spaces were plotted on a six-part map that could be linked together, it was to be discovered, by a diagram in the shape of a flying bird, close to the silhouette of a heron in flight or a flamingo in flight, or indeed any bird in flight with either long legs or a long beak or indeed, as with a stork, a long beak, a long neck and long legs. It could be seen here that the Historian Confumo was involved because it was well-known that before he announced himself to be a Historian, Confumo had been an ornithologist.**

[36] *1. A small double depression in a grey rock just big enough to receive a child's backside. The ideal space to play this game was on top of The Sprinter's Hill. A small child sitting in the depression and holding a bunch of pigeon feathers in his right hand, could imagine he was flying over the Hollery Fields. A desire to fly was scarcely ever far from any child's ambition.*

*2. A yew tree with very convenient branches for climbing if you were aged from six to ten. The aim was to reach the topmost branches carrying a bird's nest containing three eggs. Sometimes the bird's-nest was made of strips of paper ripped from a school-exercise book and the eggs were made of clotted sugar. Before a child was six year's old, the tree was considered too difficult to climb, and after ten year's old, it was considered too easy.*

*3. A mulberry tree that made an ideal climbing structure. It had been trimmed down and cut back to make way for a charnel house, and had then been dug up and re-planted with suitable straps and supports to keep it upright and flourishing in a refectory courtyard where grave-diggers ate their lunch. There was a natural platform among the topmost branches where you could juggle the Mulberry Balls.*

*4. A patch of dirty sand for building sand-castles and sand-towers with a trowel and a fork known as the King and the Queen, though few could really agree on which was which. Disagreements often ended in fights.*

*5. A small garden planted with apples on account of small children believing that to plant merely an apple-pip was not enough. "Afterall what on earth did the pip need to live on?"*

*6. A lawn for bowling. The lawn was carefully tended with close-cut grass no taller than two inches high, very green and kept very fresh. It was given to small children to keep it neat with a pair of silver scissors with wooden handles called The Snippers.*

*7. A drain pipe that took the rainwater from two gutters on a Book Depository Building and dispersed it very evenly onto three large flagstones called The Plates. A weight called The Tumbril was placed on the flagstones to see if the force of the falling water in a thunderstorm could shift it.*

**Izek Bable, the orphanage pastry-cook, formerly a soldier working with the First Encounter Artillery, was amused and delighted that the three boys, the ginger-haired Eerio Padebourne, the blonde-haired Irium Bostero and the black-haired Jendro Hisloper, had taken such an interest in his ideas about toys relevant to landscape. He volunteered to subsidize their efforts out of his pension as a retired soldier and see if he could find further funding to encourage their enthusiasms to make a collection of toys with the possibility of presenting these toys in an exhibition one day.**

CATEGORY 14. THE POST-WAR TERRITORIES TO BE SENSIBLY RECOGNISED.

**Toys, and spaces, and conditions in which to successfully play games were becoming important. It could be instructive to talk of three spaces discovered by children to play games that excited fear.**

*1. In the winter months children ran away from a triangular space of trodden snow at Fromwich Bayo which had been created by the three points marked by a broken chair, the wheel of a small cart and a large water-smoothed stone. which must have been carried some two miles from the Bayo River.*

*2. A swamp near Trodegar Garette that, it was said, sucked down babies. Children tested the lost baby theory by throwing in large stones and on occasions stealing their sisters' dolls for the experiment.*

*3. A deep pool in the River Bandon that never gave up what was thrown into it. Articles to be deliberately lost thus found a convenient home.*

## CATEGORY 15. DRAMA CONSIDERED IN THE POST-WAR PERIOD.

### Toy-associated spaces created by children to stimulate dramatic events.

*1. Tilly's Yard at Gummater Tor. A box of very fine grit called Speed-dust was kept under a wheel-less wagon in Tilly's Yard at Gummater Tor. The contents were finely sieved from dirt and sand prepared so that handfuls of it could be thrown into the air behind an upended wooden crate to pretend it was a traveling cart on a dusty road traveling fast to meet an appointment of some urgency, such as the imminent birth of a breech-baby, two lovers eloping pursued by angry parents, the death of an eminent hero who feared premature burial, or a duel between two fanatical killers armed with sharp kitchen knives. The last of these four scenarios was considered the most exciting. There was evidence to presume that the children threw the very fine dust into the air and then ran swiftly back from the scene to observe it from some thirty yards distance, to observe the fine dust cloud so created with squinted eyes, to see if they could be convinced that the effects of the dust as it spread up into the air back-lit by the sun, would suggest the crate's fast movement forward. The effect was especially exciting on a day that offered just a slight breeze. When the wind was too strong the effect was too brief and the children could not retreat back the necessary thirty yards quick enough, and therefore it was consequently disappointing.*

*2. The Tile Yard at the Paston-Cumber Northern Stables. A wooden box previously used to transport tiles was set up on stones to represent a carriage. In the absence of wheels, smeared white discs were painted at the four corners of the crate to simulate wheels in motion. The visible absence of real wheels was supplemented by the cries of children shouting abuse at invisible horses and oxen and making sounds at the back of their throats that were meant to represent the sound of four iron wheels traveling over rough ground.*

*3. A broken wooden hoop for playing Gravity-Hoop. A space between beams in a barn that suggested a cave for warring bats had an iron spar embedded in its upper east side. The hoop was to be thrown over the iron spar which was almost but not quite parallel with the ground, and driven by gravity and its own weight, gradually swung itself along the bar to fall off into the straw of the barn floor. If the spar had been parallel with the ground then there would be no movement along the spar. Sometimes this simple activity took as much as eight minutes. The winner in a game of Gravity-Hoop was the thrower who could hurl the hoop farthest up the iron spar so that it took the longest time to fall off the spike. Obviously the game involved considerable amounts of waiting time and the young contestants, especially the boys, occupied that time in searching for fleas in one another's underwear. The game was seldom played if female contestants were unavailable.*

*4. Five chairs laid out in a rough circle that could represent a meeting-place for famous people trying to settle a dispute about leadership. Five places where the game could be played were identified as disused houses in Orotarry, Peasonmost, Hastead, Junoria and Dunstan Tops. All of these disused houses had holes in the roof, apparently an important consideration.*

*5. A circular space in a fire station was set up by filling buckets with water. Every second bucket had a small hole in the bottom and when the water ran out, the game was finished. The buckets were each allotted a contestant by spinning a coin. The losers had to drink the water that remained in the unemptied buckets. To make the game more competitive, "the new bride" of the group, who was invariably the youngest girl, was persuaded to dribble a little of her spittle into each bucket. Some said it was not spittle.*

*6. A space demarcated by a pole and two blankets hanging on a washing line, that could represent a prison where important lovers could lose their heads for not saying "I love you". It was said that the game originated from the imprisonment and execution of Marlies Commendeer, the adulterous wife of a warlord living in Paston Threes before the Black Horse Sundown Skirmish.*

*7. Two horse blankets and a loaf of stale bread set on a stool arranged to represent a misunderstood love story by children whose parents had separated over a dispute about money. The blankets stood in for a bed and the bread stood in for the lost or stolen money. The children harangued the bread on the stool for being deceitful and ended their game by jumping on the bed to destroy the evil responsible for the arguments between much loved but now missing parents. The quality of the game was measured in the number of tears shed, by both boys as well as girls. It was a very emotional game and played as little as possible because it was so distressful.*

**CATEGORY 16. LOCAL CONSIDERATIONS IN THE TERRITORIES.**

## Still smaller landscape toy-spaces.

*1. A corner between the out-of-school latrines and a park wall. It was used for playing marbles. It sloped a little from east to west and from north to south with a larger depression in the centre left and a smaller depression in the centre right. Calculations of long standing and passed down by small children could enable the glass balls to run in trajectories that would appear to be contradictory but that would inevitably end up in wins.*

*The best time to use the space was when it had been raining for an hour and then superficially swiftly dried by a warm wind making the surface of the stone slightly tacky so that the marbles dragged a little. This dragging was perceptible to children familiar with the space and delighted them by appearing to make the marbles travel in apparent slow motion.*

*2. A stone platform some twelve inches high, two yards across and four yards long, built with the intention of supporting a bronze equestrian statue. The platform was never used for such, the bronze being melted down to make cannon-balls for a war over a jealous painter suspected of sabotage in the cause of the secret burning of a painting of a popular politician. A war that was never in the end resolved. The stone was soft, and after many years had begun to flake due to frost erosion. Children sitting round its edges had, over time, polished the flaking stone with their shufflings, making the runnels and depressions smooth for imaginative play with marbles, bread pellets, toothpicks, dice, balls of mud and dead creatures like beetles, caterpillars, and even sometimes, lizards and mice.*

*3. A slope of beaten earth tamped down hard by running and walking feet and ideal for small-ball games like Tip-gloss, Partridge, Pleasing-Mary, Toss-pot, Pass the Parcel Please, Chimes, Speed-end, Sixes, Climb the Mountain, In-China, Ladies-man and Grips and Gripes.*

*4. A slope of short sheep-cropped grass ending in a depression backed by a grass mound. The slope was ideal for rolling down, since the depression and then the mound would act as safety brakes.*

*5. A stretch of carpet coloured blue with an inserted orange panel. This carpet of unknown origin but probably manufactured in the South and brought North on camel-back, now covered some forty square yards of the Community Hall floor in Addaminta. Children played Roundamentine on its comforting surface, and parents, chewing blueberries and drinking yarrowroot-water, made a habit of sitting around its edges on three-legged milking stools whilst their infants played.*

*6. A section of pine floor-boards in a corridor of four openings in the Mancil Town House lead to unused cupboards whose doors, through shrinkage caused by flooding, had gaps of some two inches between the bottom of every door and the floor. Children had given the cupboards numbers, not necessarily in the traditional chronology, and a game of marbles had developed where accumulated throws could be amassed to provide winners and losers using the under-door spaces.*

*7. A rectangular space was contested by boys in Erminatory between four horse chestnut trees where leaves collected. When the wind was in a certain direction in September through to early December, between the departure of the swallows and the arrival of the first frosts, it created closely contained whirlpools of tree litter that could not escape out of the rectangle This event mesmerized the children who believed that the leaves were propelled by governed forces that could be ordered if only you knew the trick of how to do so. For boys, success earned you heroic advantages with female company. Growing a moustache signalled the end of the right to perform, though sticklers for the magic of the game persisted, surreptitiously borrowing their fathers' shaving equipment to be certain of passing the no-moustaches test.*

*8. A heavy brown blanket belonging to the children of the Artillery Contingent in Arkinsor that smelt of horse urine and dried porridge, had four vertical rips, three natural from boisterous play and one made with a knife, and three burn holes made with hot coals falling out of the fire. The whole made a map of a foreign country that children – many of them missing a father killed in battle - could see was full of thick forests and safe places to hide from loneliness, melancholia and empty stomachs. Children waited for hours for a missing parent to return. And of course, they never did.*

**Whilst the children played games of territory in miniature with counters, playing-cards, dead insects and painted pebbles, they were knowingly or unknowingly mocking or copying their elders who were squabbling over real landscape territories after years of wars where nearly every yard had been eagerly disputed.**

*9. A section of miniature garden in a horse trough. Stones, gravel, earth, moss and small plants had gathered there over a period of time such as to invite Smallack and Timorous, two children of the large Mallamy family to make tracks with two index fingers to represent the roads from PastonCumber to Akinadower, and inhabit a cave of tumbled stones with a damson pip identifying the elder child and a sycamore wing identifying the younger.*

*10. In the Sleeping-Room at the Cradlemouth Nursery which was the home of the Sheepless Hunt, there were eight large and heavy red horse-rugs sewn together with fishing-twine and habitually called the Ruby Cumulus. The rugs were invariably infested with small children because the rugs made very good miniature mountains whilst the children awaited their parents to stop hunting the fox. Worried mothers looking for missing children after dark always made it their first port of call to search. Sometimes very small children gave up trying to burrow their way out of the heavy ruby-red folds and were found curled up fast and blissfully asleep, left-hand fingers in their mouths and with the red furry cloth clutched in their right hands. They invariably dreamt of family reunions.*

*11. A large white rounded boulder. It had been deeply scratched by ice action and had been dropped by an ancient melting glacier. It was now positioned in a very large and empty field of grass. For ten days every hot August it was covered in small red mites eating the moss and lichen that covered the boulder, and every February it was used by sheep as a shelter out of the wind and snow. It was the center of a children's game called*

*Laseroque where the boulder was beaten with willow sticks and called upon to open up and display its secrets about harbouring small red lambs.*

*Smellett said the local people were keen to make an association between the mites and the sheep to help explain the rock's strange isolation in the centre of the large field. And they once believed that the rock could surely be opened like a trunk or a box along one of its deep glacier scratches. The local children had taken the mystery of the boulder very seriously.*

*Axelot suggested the mite and the sheep might not be entirely unrelated since the sheep droppings that had fallen in the shadow of the rock created ideal circumstances for the incubation for the mites that appeared in their thousands in the month of August. What puzzled him was the exact seven months that separated the flourishing of the mites and the sheltering of the sheep. Conceivably any winter month from November round till March could have sheltered sheep, and any summer month from June until September could have encouraged the mites. He began to believe that there was a relationship between mites and sheep that was triggered by the quality of the rock itself. Each succeeding generation of local people believed less in any magic properties and their original beliefs degenerated into a children's game where the word Laseroque had evolved from an imperfectly heard version of Glacier Rock. The historian Eeleye Nollkeins disagreed about using the word "degenerated" in such a context arguing that the beliefs had been enlivened and consolidated resulting in an enrichment of thinking and not a degeneration.*

*12. At Framistower there was a river-washed flat rock pitted with shallow depressions the size of a child's palm. The depressions had been created by freshwater clams, generation after generation. The children filled the depressions with their spittle, watching its tiny bubbles be washed away at the next downpour of rain which was frequent.*

*13. In an abandoned builder's yard used as a dump was a large pile of powdered chalkstone laid out on flagstones. The white dust was so finely powdered, it blew away in the wind. Children wrote their names in the flat white powder whilst making a wish that had to involve an understanding of Goodness. "I have been good today because I washed my hands with soap and water." "I have been good today because I did not shout at my grandfather at having bones in his leg which stopped him from playing Saucers and Plates with me." "I have been good today about not peeing on the cat who scratched me."*

*14. There was a two-metre square flagstone in the PastonCumber Southern Suburbs, at the conjuction of Stringwater Street and The Calling Card. Young people often stopped by to snatch a kiss. It was generally considered a forbidden gesture but if you did it swiftly with closed eyes and no discernable fumbling hand, you might get away with it.*

*The flagstone was regularly covered with bird lime, sticky feathers and small sticks in the Spring nesting season from birds nesting in the walnut trees above. Occasionally a small dead unfeathered nestling might be discovered there in the early weeks of June. On the first day of August, local children tidied up the space, burying any dead birds, and they washed the flagstone clean of avian debris. Some local people called the first day of August Birdfall Day.*

## CATEGORY 17. CONSIDERING THE DETAILS OF PEACE.

**Very small landscape toys. Here were four games to be played on portable surfaces.**

*1. A circular worn breadboard used by "the baker of boys", Yolaf Shires, to play Flags, a game of flapping shadows.*

*2. A butcher's chopping block covered in dried pig's blood was used to play "The Hogs" a game sometimes called Whirrals by girls from the South who were allowed to uncover their hair when their mothers were not looking.*

[46] *3. An anvil reputed to be instrumental for the making of swords where savage cuts in the iron were claimed to be the results of heroes rehearsing great deeds.*

*This anvil, far too heavy to move without horses, was kept by the granite water trough in Arminteer where domestic animals came to drink and subsequently urinate on the anvil. The children enjoyed the smell of the urine on the iron and had invented a game called Master and Mistresses.*

*4. A chopping board in the orphan's kitchen at Freset, by common mythology used by the cooks to scare children. It was said that the very deep cuts had been made by chopping off the thumbs of small children who refused to stop sucking their thumbs passed their third birthday.*

## CATEGORY 18. OBSESSING THE DETAILS OF PEACE.

### Further Landscape Board-Game toys.

*1. A white-painted board marked up in thirty-six equal squares on which red and black counters could be moved on the spin of a dice, square by square, in any direction to eliminate the field of play for your opposing player. Once a square has been landed upon it could not be landed on again, and for convenience, was marked with a pencil, crayon, adhesive paper, or any other suitable marker. In some competitions it has been known that the forbidden squares have been indicated by biscuit crumbs, coffee-stains marked with the rounded base of the coffee cup, small denomination coins, leaves of a privet hedge, coal-dust, guano and dead beetles whose legs had been removed in case the beetles came alive again and scuttled off.*

*The origin of the game is supposedly based on a landscape, namely the white salt pans of Ridley not infrequently washed over by a swollen river whose waters were coloured by thousands of freshwater shrimps.*

*2. A very favoured game much played for high stakes and considerable honour was called The Fox. It was played around a painted board where the colour of the thirty-six squares in a configuration of six by six is probably immaterial, but the sentence which contains all the letters of the alphabet is essential.* THE QUICK BROWN FOX JUMPS OVER THE LAZY DOG *is written sequentially in the squares, leaving the thirty-sixth square to be marked with a full stop. All the twenty-six letters of the alphabet in this sentence have to be accommodated by the dice-throws cast in alphabetical order. The combined letters A and Z in the word "lazy", being the first and last letters of the alphabet, were considered auspicious and the fortunate caster of the dice that created this result was permitted to be idle for twenty-six throws. If this happened three times, the caster was considered the winner. This state of affairs always apparently favoured female players so much so that young ambitious males dressed up in skirts and bodices to play the game. The last letter of the sentence is "dog" which is "god" spelled backward and has to be avoided at all costs.*

*3. There was a table-top in a PastonCumber Drinking House store-room scratched by wire coat hangers, marked by hot pewter beakers, a burning tobacco pipe, a collar-and-cuffs iron, a serrated bread knife and a pointed tool that could have been a gimlet, but was more likely to be a corkscrew. The table was also scratched in parallel lines with maybe the metal clasps of a brassiere worn by a woman resting on her back weighted down by unknown pressure. During daylight hours when drinking was not permitted, children played racing coin games on the table-top, the larger heavier coins along the groves, the smaller lighter coins laid over the circular burn-marks. As soon as twilight approached and five stars had appeared in the sky, the children were swiftly ejected and heavy drinkers with their wives took over the space to entertain themselves with everything that alcohol could encourage.*

[48] *4. A simple patterned rug in the entrance hall to the Gosthought Armory made good mountains when heavy books from the military library were stacked underneath.*

**And so the number of toys in terms of several categories certainly including the space-games was increasing. Space-games were copied from location to location, village to village and town to town, all more or less the same in essence, but different according to the differences in landscape characteristics.**

**Jendro Hisloper and Irium Bostero and Eerio Padebourne were indeed war orphans. In the blossoming peace-time, Izek Bable was the orphanage pastry-cook. Formerly he had been an artillery soldier ever since war started three decades previously. His passion was maps which demanded in utilitarian usage to aid the establishment of military positions, both aggressive and defensive. Where to situate ambushes. Where to initiate ideal theatres of skirmish. How to use the landscape in fact for military advantage. He enjoyed landscape and the mapping of it, even, given sufficient men and materials, of how he might design it. He had moved in peace-time from modeling landscapes to modeling pastries. The inferences contained in that move cannot be downplayed. But the miniaturization is relevant. His military experiences and his general curiosity about landscape phenomena and its influence on human activity had persuaded him that what he really would like to concern himself with was the writing of History. Like so many others, he wanted to be a Historian.**

**Although it could have been Izek Bable who led the three boys Jendro Hisloper and Irium Bostero and Eerio Padebourne to become interested in board games, through his own fascination with maps, Eerio thought about these miniature landscape situations and came to realize it seemed to satisfy a sort of curious desire to be settled and wanted. It gave him a space to live in that could be controlled. Staring at a tabletop, a rumpled carpet, a half-destroyed billiard table, the broken tiles of a latrine floor, even a breadboard ferociously cut and**

scraped by a breadknife, he could imagine his father and often himself, running for cover, fleeing before panicked horses, hoping to kiss a decorated woman or rescue a lost cousin. He frequently fell asleep feeling he was an ant in a hailstorm, a wounded fish in a mill-stream, a leaf falling over a waterfall.

To keep disciplined control of their collection of toys, the three war-orphans, Jendro Hisloper and Irium Bostero and Eerio Padebourne had every item ticketed. The tickets were made out in long hand with black ink on card attached to the relevant item with a white thread.

Izek Bable suggested to the children that they should show their collection of toys to the orphanage steward, Opsinger Dedestry, who was an amateur archivist and a musician who specialized in military music. Opsinger Dedestry suggested that the three war-orphans, Jendro Hisloper and Irium Bostero and Eerio Padebourne, should build a collection of musical toys. When put together, these musical instruments, suitably adapted, might make a sit-down orchestra, to play music suitable for peacetime.

# MUSIC: SQUEALERS

### CATEGORY 19. LOOKING TO SETTLE ANIMOSITIES WITH MUSIC.

Squealer instruments that might be usefully employed to make an orchestra whose specialty in war-time celebrations had required much boisterous noise.

> *1. "A blade of dried Page-grass held firmly in a fork of wood to be blown by the mouth so that it vibrates. If blown well and hard, it could make sounds that may be described as somewhere between a howl and a screech. After about ten blows of the mouth you have to change the grass, but Page-grass grows very*

*freely in the Hollery Hills." Five children with hearing impairments sat on a Hollery Hill and practiced blowing Page-grass together with dubious results. Washerwomen often ordered them to move on, the noise was so irritating.*

*2. A strip of slate fashioned in a triangular shape that when scratched with a piece of chalk makes a painful squealing or screeching sound that can be made governable by an expert. Experts were not easy to find. And if they were found, they were often reluctant to educate children, believing that the hideous noise they could make had powers which could be subverted to ignominious ends.*

*3. A section of mirror bordered with a wooden frame so that you do not cut your fingers. When this mirror is rubbed with a wet finger, it can be made to produce a high-pitched squeal or screech, which in skilled hands can be played higher or lower in timbre. The finger should be moistened in such a way as to produce the maximum satisfactory sound; too moist and the gesture becomes mute, too dry and the finger does not slip.*

*4. A length of piping that when twirled around your head, can be made to produce a squealing sound. Twirling faster increases the pitch. The sound can be regulated by the twirling speed and by the size of the aperture of the pipe.*

## Squealer Instruments to play softer music.

*1. A tin-whistle as small as a low denomination coin, to be placed in the mouth between teeth and lips, on which to blow and suck. The sound produced is small but potentially musical. It suggests the song of the night-bird called a Crail, sometimes spelt Crawel or even Craal if you lived just South of the North-South Dividing Line.*

*2. A whistle shaped like a crescent moon that produces a soft rustling sound ending in a thin screech. The sound can be reliably repeated, so a looping oscillating round of sound is often played. Some people think of it as a percussion instrument, but a player cannot strike many variations out of the noise, so its use is limited.*

## Squealer Instruments to be played in an aggressive military marching band.

*1. A wooden pipe with seven finger-holes attached to a bellows to be held under the arm and pumped. Some say it originated as a mature instrument in the North, but was considered to be too ungovernable and too childish to produce serious music further South, hence it was regulated to the nursery. In the cacophony of a marching band, it could be used as a shrill instrument to scare the enemy, and by its squealing, can certainly be heard a great way off.*

*2. A short tin whistle capable of producing only one note. It often comes attached to a spirally folded length of gut or parchment spring-strengthened by a wire coil, tipped with a dyed feather. When the whistle is blown, the wire coil unwinds, the gut or parchment extends and the feather quivers. It is a called a "cheeper" though its sound is harsh and arresting, and more related to a screech. It should really be called a "screecher".*

## Squealer Instruments to be played by day.

*1. A fat-bellied wooden instrument, gaudily painted with nursery scenes and provided with a handle which when turned produces simple melodies. Some say the sounds are beautiful and evocative, others say that the sounds are no more evocative than the sad cries of a cat being strangled. Either way, the squealing and screeching produced by the instrument can be regulated by the use of a file or rasp on a series of tines within the instrument's interior, and musical notation can be made relevant enough for a sympathetic player to follow a written score in the company of others.*

[52] *2. Several compound bladders sewn together from a pig's intestine with stout pine-bark thread; any other thread would rapidly corrode with the contact with the acidic skin of the intestines. The bladder farts, screeches and squeals can only sensibly be used in sardonic musical compositions.*

## Squealer Instruments to make a piece of music to be played at night in the open air.

*1. Yellow five-fingered whistles A group of female orphans under eight year's old had found a way of grieving about their loss of parents. They sang lullabys and nursery songs whose meaning they did not fully understand. What was a "cradle"? What was a "bough"? What was "bunting"? Who were "the sleepers in clover"? But they had soothing rhythms that they sung in primitive unison and they were a comfort if you had trouble falling asleep. Most orphans had trouble falling asleep, so often haunted by nightmares. Izek Bable, the orphanage pastry-cook, found the children a collection of wooden whistles from a pre-war bandstand cellar. The orphans painted them yellow and sat by candlelight playing at night in an apple orchard in September. Every now and then a ripe apple would fall out of a tree and startle the children as it hit the ground, such that they should start the piece of music they were playing all over again. This activity became more frequent in October and one of their number built the activity into a long piece of music called The Falling Apples. This became refined into Red Falling Apple Music and Green Falling Apple Falling Music. Touched by their sincerity in playing, the group soon had admirers. One such group who were a little older and had been carried in scorched blankets from the Fire of Glitzover, copied these original players. They painted their whistles orange, a darker colour than yellow to demonstrate their seniority in age and maybe reflect their brush with flames.*

*2. A child's carpenter's saw with a painted wooden handle which, when stroked with a bow, can be made to make melodious noises that are evocative of night animals and can be heard a great way off. The children who managed to make interesting noises from the sawing sound, ignored the abuse shouted at them and played at the top of their strength till all the cats in the vicinity disappeared and there was, it is said, a plague of mice.*

### Squealer Instruments to look good, if not sound so good, in an orchestral performance.

*1. A miniature wooden and brass machine with pipes decorated with coloured stars, intended to be hung above a baby's cradle. It could be said by the imaginative that the instrument looked like an extravagant miniature castle, and could, with wind being blown into the pipes, be made to make noises that might be associated with squealing, but the volume was poor and the sounds were difficult to regulate.*

*2. A white porcelain animal dotted with stars that could look maybe like a pig, that responded with a squealing noise when blown through the snout. Melba Goering cradled it and strangely called it "her mother". She lulled herself to sleep with the instrument, and its smell clung to her, making her a pariah. Her father avoided her, being reluctant to eat in her presence for fear of infection. Such behavior was not to be considered at all sympathetic in a father.*

# MUSIC: RATTLERS

#### CATEGORY 20. MUSIC AS A TRUSTFUL PANACEA.

### Rattler Instruments for a virtuoso orchestra whose speciality was celebrations.

*1. A discrete affair of wooden boxes filled with various sized beans and peas. Great care was expended on the exterior decoration of the boxes. The blonde-haired child Grappy*

*Melidorus had a mind for business and set up a stall to make multiple copies of the decorated rattlers which he sold. He commissioned his sister Harrio to create a maintenance unit so that none of his products in the hands of his relatives and friends ever looked untidy, unkempt or disheveled. It has to be admitted that the exterior painted decoration had much greater value than the sound the instrument made, even in the hands of children who practiced continuously day and night.*

*2. Three strips of wood attached at one end by a leather strap. The three Casterly children made themselves a small accomplished orchestral band and, dressed in red coats and red boots, serenaded the streets where they lived alongside their grandparents and their animals. The animals enjoyed the noise and joined in with appropriate howlings and barkings.*

**Rattler Instruments to play soft music.**

*1. A parchment cylinder filled with grass seed, and sealed with wax, often used to imitate the sound of rain. On every week-ending ready for celebration, Polly Mistral made a new one. Her friends ordered her to desist because playing the instrument invariably brought on the rain that always messed up their hair.*

*2. A sealed cardboard box filled with poppy seeds "stolen from a baker", designed to be shaken to soothe a young child to fall asleep. Crespi called it a "sheela". No one knew where she got that name from but her father said he had heard it down South. "Down South" to Crespi somehow seemed to be underground and she dug pits for her "sleeping box" where the soil was sandy. Sometimes Crespi forgot where she had buried her sheela and she panicked and would not stop screaming, and the whole household had to take up shovels and start digging.*

**Rattler Instruments to be played in an aggressive military band.**

*1. A collection of wooden tines and metal strikers, all painted yellow, which when shaken and rolled around an axis on a handle, produce a loud, strident and irritating repetitious sound to be heard a great way off. Such an instrument is often found at ball games.*

*2. A box of small stones gathered in a quarry. Gracious Dedrict hid it under her wooden bed and only brought it out when the moon was shining.*

*3. A dried gourd partially filled with dried beans. Originally there were at least a thousand beans in the gourd, but Assisis, the instrument player, becoming hungry, opened the gourd and, stealing a few beans, ate them surreptitiously. After several weeks the instrument, due to Assisi's hunger, was down to some one hundred beans and the instrument could not make enough noise to satisfy audiences and it was abandoned.*

**Rattler Instruments to be played in a sit-down orchestra.**

*1. A sockle given to children in the South at their naming ceremonies. It is traditionally a long wooden cylinder with a circle of parchment stretched over either end. The intention is to continually tip the sockle from side to side to reproduce the sound of rain, running water and hail-stones on glass.*

**Rattler Instruments to make music to be played at night in the open air.**

*1. A globe of porcelain containing pieces of coloured glass.*

*2. A sphere of wood containing dried peas.*

*3. A sphere of wood containing dried beans.*

*4. A wooden sphere containing "rushaway" seed-pods.*

**Rattler Instruments to look good, if not sound so good, in an orchestral performance.**

*1. Four painted china spheres mounted on a rack. It is suggested that the rattling sound within the spheres could be made with grated talc, though no-one wished to smash the delicate china spheres to find out.*

# MUSIC: BANGERS

## CATEGORY 21. IF MUSIC BE THE FOOD OF LOVE AS A PANACEA

*1. Hollow sticks to be struck with other hollow sticks. Heartbeats were to be considered as an inspiration.*

*2. Hollow gourds to be beaten with a cane.*

*3. There was a swaggering mob of adolescent males who wore black with crimson trimmings and who disdained sweet bird-song. They elevated rooks and crows, ravens and callous jackdaws to high and harsh cackling vocal significance. They played drums and they banged brassware. They risked calls of effeminacy by not cutting their nails and painting them black. Their frontman was a dandy called Pie. His detractors called him Maggie Pie. Collectively they had a display that impressed strangers. When met in solitary fashion they were shabby and seen to be covered in damp spit which was not their own and preferably female and most desirably, it was rumoured came from a pregnant whore. Nobody believed this of course. First of all it was not too easy to find a pregnant whore. It was rumoured that they kept a pregnant whore in chains for this purpose. That was also a sensational story that nobody believed. They mostly called themselves the Daws, in emulation, it was said of jackdaws.*

*4. The Blind Band were often not blind at all but wore smoked glass spectacles, as did their audiences who copied or sported black eye patches or else tattooed their eye-sockets. The T-Cup*

*Musicians had never drunk tea. There was also an Open-Mouthed Fish Band.*

**Banger Instruments to play soft music.**

*1. A drum made of stretched paper to be beaten with a feather.*

*2. A drum made of stretched parchment to be beaten with a hot spoon.*

*3. Empty walnuts shells on a string.*

**Banger Instruments to be played in an aggressive military band.**

*1. A drum with a pig-skin to be banged with a stick.*

*2. A drum with a parchment skin to be beaten with a deer-bone bone.*

*3. A drum with a cow-hide skin stretched over a wooden barrel to be carried with a strap over the musician's shoulder.*

*4. A tin drum. To accompany the drum-beats, Gunter Tainly, a natural baritone, learnt to sing high and his sister, Sema, a soprano, learnt to sing low.*

*5. A tin drum accompanied by castanets.*

*6. Hinged clappers.*

*7. Hand clappers.*

**Banger Instruments to be played in a sit-down orchestra.**

*1. A wooden rack with ten canes of different lengths to be beaten with a wooden stick.*

*2. A bell-rack.*

*3. A bell-rack with ropes. Players sat in a small circle and lulled all the listening babies to sleep. They hired themselves out playing lullabys.*

**Banger Instruments to make music to be played at night in the open air.**

*1. Water-glasses.*

*2. A bell-chime.*

**Banger Instruments to look good, if not sound so good, in an orchestral performance.**

*1. A machine with hinges.*

*2. A round bowl filled with water and mounted on a chest of drawers veneered with silver-birch bark.*

# MUSIC: BLOWERS

### CATEGORY 22. HOPEFULLY LOOKING TO SETTLE ANIMOSITIES WITH MUSIC.

**Blower Instruments for a virtuoso orchestra whose specialty tended to be celebrations like marriages and births.**

*1. A pipe called an Eight-Holer was created by Paling Stresser. Few could appreciate the newly fashioned instrument. It certainly sounded unusual but it was noticed that local birds took to copying the noise. As far away as Trutle there were large aggressive black birds that nested in the elms and apparently taught their fledglings to imitate the new music.*

*2. A pipe called a Red Face invented by Teddeo Possum. He had a red face from blowing his whistle and the red face, once stimulated, never diminished. Teddeo was called "the boy with the red face" and had a following. Twenty drummers with red-painted faces patrolled the district whenever they were permitted.*

*3. A horn. The horn-players stole butter to grease their fingers to permit a sound-spillage. They were frequently arrested. Butter was expensive.*

*4. A bugle. Six boys who came together to play curlies against a brick wall at Fenly Streams made a bugle band. The sound improved when Izek Bable, the pastry cook, let them practice in his white-tiled pantry where he baked Samartines full of currants of which the six boys feasted themselves until they vomited over their fancy shirts and shat in their canvas breeches.*

*Opsinger Dedestry wanted them to play marching songs – but they had had enough of marching - their fathers had marched here and there and back again and returning as like as not with bloody noses and bloody clothes, splattering their blood on kitchen floors to the screams of kitchen-women. They did not wish to be associated with all that again. They sat in a sycamore tree and invented what they called "a slow sitting march."*

*The women from the hot-roast kitchen crocheted woolen hats to avoid the draughts coming from the cold-meats room. Cooking and music became an entity. The orphans wore white with blue shoes with yellow laces. They painted portraits of their parents, though most of them had never seen their parents. Some had a reminiscence of a mother. Some pretended they had a remembrance of a father and painted their fathers looking like bugles with gold tassels for hair.*

**Blower Instruments to play soft music.**

*1. A wooden comb and a sheet of tissue paper.*

*2. Blower Instruments to be played in an aggressive military band.*

[60] *3. An exceedingly long muted brass trumpet supporting a flag.*

**Blower Instruments to be played in a sit-down orchestra.**

*1. A metal tube mounted on a decorated wooden box.*

*2. Straws blown in water.*

**Blower Instruments to make music to be played at night in the open air.**

*1. A glass trumpet decorated with painted flowers.*

**Blower Instruments to look good, if not sound so good, in an orchestral performance.**

*1. A collection of welded brass pipes wound around each other like golden snakes.*

**Opsinger Dedestry set himself to make a collection of whistles as a new contribution to the toys collection, to flesh out the category of musical toys.**

*1. A dried pea in a length of bamboo.*

*2. In the shape of a singing bird painted yellow – perhaps like a canary.*

*3. Made of rolled tin lacquered in fish-oil.*

*4. Made of brass and very heavy; believed to have been in the possession of a policeman.*

*5. Made of ceramic in such a fashion as to warble.*

*6. To be filled with water.*

*7. Teak bound with brass rings.*

*8. In the shape of a penis.*

*9. Curled like a butterfly's proboscis.*

*10. Made of rolled tin with seven finger-holes. Polotter whistled every time he picked it up and expected it to whistle back to him. He fashioned it a mouth with two purple-red lips held in a kissing mode.*

*11. Inscribed with a motto –" Blow me and I'll fly to you."*

*12. A short flute.*

*13. A carved acorn still in its cup.*

All this interest in music for peacetime was productive. Many musical instruments had been collected. The overall count of toys was rapidly growing. The district South of PastonCumber was full of music festivals. Opsinger Dedestry made certain that he was credited with their creation. The three boys, though irritated by Dedestry's claims, swallowed their irritation and did their best to demonstrate their gratitude and they moved on. What this music did accomplish was to renew an interest in birds, which the disturbances of the wars had diminished. Birds flying through the air at the start of the wars became such valuable targets for sling-shot experiments, that their numbers soon diminished.

Then the interest in birds encouraged an interest in flying. The boys concentrated for a time on finding and discovering and repairing toys that had bird associations. The unused scullery at the Wouverain Orphanage was getting congested with toys and Izek Bable started to search for a larger space to house them. He found an unused weapons storage bunker outside Ward Fifty-Nine. It had no windows but it was dry, had wooden floors, a second storey and a flat roof. It was rarely visited and Izek Bable arranged a reliable security system. The three boys and Izek were the only persons to possess keys.

Whilst this little world of war-toys, Wouverain orphanages, and Historians' rivalry was continuing, local Greater Continental

[62] activities persisted. There was a fire started by a rat-catcher which consumed a suburb of PastonCumber killing some three hundred citizens, including nearly seventy children under six years old. "It was one way to reduce the shame of so many orphans", said the cynical Oliver Openharass. There was a plague whose symptoms were blindness, boils in the armpit and groin and erotic hallucinations. It decimated the villages of Dieppedoral. There was an assassination in Transmittra of the Benefactor and his child wife which scandalized the Lower Eastside of Scrutiny Fielding, the town where the best steel knives were manufactured. There was an earthquake which killed off the families of the Semester House and the Ridgery, and a befouling of the River Calderine, believed to be caused by swine fever which carried off seven orphanages and their human contents with its effluvia. There was a goldrush in the South-West which lead to savage repressive laws on meetings of over ten citizens that are still in the law books. And greed and a desire for red cloth closed down the maze of communication roads around Aldenbasery that triggered a financial recession and left an area of five thousand acres of good arable land unharvested.

There was a manifestation of superstition created by the guilt of injuring some thirty children in the forest of Twickery. And an expedition to the North was wiped out in unseasonal blizzards along the Diepeer Divide. There was an invasion of troops demanding linguistic parity which paralyzed the county of Trimea for a while. There was rumoured to be a drought which devastated the South-Eastern borders with no rainfall for five years that seems to have wiped out a slew of animals including the White Sloth, the Bucking Ibex, the Emerald-necked Cassowary, the Coxen Obnough and the flocks of Passerole Eider-Duck which fifty years ago, it is said, could hide the sun for two days flying across the sky in their seasonal migrations.

Opsinger Dedestry, the Wouverain Orphanage Director, saw an opportunity to better himself at the children's expense by recreating himself as a Historian applying for funds to further the children's research. Opsinger Dedestry envied the Historian Lutumariner whose career had won him prestige as a scholar, as an expert on the three decades of war and as an authority looked up to for his organizing abilities. At first Lutumariner was almost entirely ignorant of Dedestry's ambitious nature, but that was to change. An antagonism both occupational, but also very personal, was to develop between the two men.

Whilst waiting for the funding application to be processed, the small company of the three orphans, the ginger-haired Eerio Padebourne, the blonde-haired Irium Bostero, and the black-haired Jendro Hisloper, had simply collected what was available, what had come their way, what could be discovered, what could be found. Then perhaps too readily the boys had been persuaded to develop the suggestions of others, first by Izek Bable, the pastry-cook, as regards to Toy Games, and then by the Director of the Wouverain Orphanage, Opsinger Dedestry with reference to Musical Toys. Both subject matters had been accepted with alacrity and the relevant collections pursued. But perhaps led by Eerio, there was a feeling that the boys' subjectivity was to be the leading factor in the Toys Project, otherwise the identity of the project might get diverted and become a project devised by adults of an older generation whose major life experience was too much bound up in the experience of the wars.

Perhaps influenced by the flocks of the disappearing Passerole Eider-Duck whose presence in the wild fifty years ago, could hide the sun for two days, had an influence, certainly on the black-haired boy, Jendro Hisloper. Jendro's long dead father, retiring from being an artillery marksman in the Summary Regiments of Aquabuster, who had been reluctant to put down his musket and who regularly fed the Senior wards of the Orphange with duck-meat, needed to be remembered. Jendro turned his attention to the empty skies and suggested they should search for flying toys.

# [64] FLYING

### CATEGORY 23 HOPEFULLY LOOKING TO THE SKY.

## Flying toys.

*1. An artificial bird on a string. The string ran through its eyes. Both of the eyes. "I usually flew it on the PastonCumber Heath." Amy Scribbant said, "That was where the winds were so dependably good." And as the bird landed on the grass, she ran to pick it up and hug it to her chest with tears in her bright eyes.*

*2. An artificial damselfly on a string. "The difference between a dragonfly and a damselfly is not restricted to the size of either of them." Comely Sanders said defiantly, expecting to be corrected.*

*3. A kite fashioned in the shape of a bird. The bird was a fantasy related to no known* species. *"I kept it because I could never throw anything away."*

*4. A kite fashioned in the shape of a bat. It is debatable that the child who owned this toy knew the difference between a bird and a bat. "A bat was a bird who flew at night," she said. The young female in question who made this suggestion was Poplara Evens whose mother was a seamstress working on an embroidery depicting the Battle of the Assault at Devis Top where the loser of the battle famously was killed with an arrow in his eye. Though that was unproven because the embroidery was ambiguous at this point. The winner of the battle was a tyrant who slashed at the world with a sadism that frightened the country until his death. His funeral was well remembered. His large decomposing corpse was too large for his coffin. The corpse had to have its legs broken to make the corpse fit. All who tried to squeeze the body into the coffin's narrow space, it is said, stank with its decomposition until their own dying day. Ivory Chess, Poplara's illegitimate cousin was cynically amused and had the words "A bat is not a bird" tattooed on Poplara's stomach when it came to have Poplara's body entombed. Ivory*

*Chess charged money to view this naïve observation in its faded blue ink. He amassed a fortune.*

*5.Sycamore seed wings painted with eyes. Agrimony Tisslouser had ten of these sycamore seed wings. They were sticky from his holding them in his fingers for so long before offering them to the black-haired boy Jendro Hisloper to add to his collection.*

*6. A thrown toad. "You seize the unsuspecting toad by its back legs and throw it over your left shoulder with your right hand." And she demonstrated this activity, being apparently unaware of the toad's discomfort.*

*7. A sheet with four knotted corners. Some said each knotted corner held a cherry stone. The trick was to get the cherry stones all the same weight otherwise the sheet would bloated land on the ground unevenly. She tried peach stones and apricot stones but found them too heavy. She was reluctant to give up the peach stones because she was very fond of eating peaches. Opsinger Dedestry was aware of this and bought her peaches to attempt to seduce her.*

*8. A balloon tied to a long string and kept up in the sky perpetually by a strong west wind. It was there for at least three weeks. When the wind finally changed direction and veered towards the South, the frayed string could not accept the new demands of the wind-change and it snapped. The balloon escaped towards the South. It was last seen as a small red dot rushing away over a forest of dead trees whose roots had perished by being covered in brackish water due to unseasonal flooding.*

*9. A slow fuse tied to a kite. When the fuse was exhausted the kite burst into flames in the sky over Skittle Moor and entertained the local villagers. The kite fell to the ground and set alight a hay-rick belonging to a farmer who had a heart condition who demanded compensation for his discomfort.*

**At Marley it became fashionable for a time for the citizens to fly their clothing. Local drapers made a small profit for trading**

[66] **in cast-off clothing on windy days. They were like those umbrella-sellers exploiting days of sudden showers.**

*10. A shirt with an open neck and the buttons undone, flying as a kite.*

*11. A large clean handkerchief initialled with the letter F. F is for Flying.*

*12. A hat, a blouse and then a petticoat flying as a kite, flown by a girl overcome by her ambition to fly all the clothes in her wardrobe.*

*13. Mattie Blokers shivered on the ground as her clothes flew in the air.*

**In an attempt to fill the skies with flying toys, young children began to throw objects into the air on days of high wind. By weighing them down and variously balancing them with grit and sand, after much practice, they were able to direct their kites to selected targets, encouraging them for example, to crash to the ground before the feet of unwary pedestrians. The grass was littered with crashed toys.**

**The ginger-haired Eerio Padebourne, the blonde-haired Irium Bostero and the black-haired Jendro Hisloper were determined to collect as many variables as possible in each toy category until questions were beginning to be asked if this was wise. Storage spaces were starting to be difficult to find, and it has to be confessed that the repetitions were now often difficult to differentiate. It started to make sections of their collection often perhaps tedious.**

CATEGORY 24. BURNT FLYING TOYS RESCUED FROM THE AIR.

**This is a list of a collection of burnt toys rescued from the air. The night flying of kites became fashionable. Small children set**

**their kites alight for entertainment. The charred remains were carefully collected and in some cases the toy was restored. Many of these burnt toys were beyond repair, but the blonde-haired Irium Bostero was convinced that in certain cases the skill and imagination in the evidence seen at their restoration were worth recording, and he had the engineer and draughtsman Periculum Arrestes commissioned to make replicas or drawings of these burnt toys. Ginger-haired Eerio Padebourne, after some reflection, accepted them as being legitimate for his collection.**

*1. A paper and cardboard kite made from an unwrapped paper funnel.*

*2. A string bag made from short sections of the string used by the PastonCumber postal services.*

*3. A collection of pigeon feathers strapped to lead weights.*

*4. A ball of paper wings.*

*5. A discarded wood ant's nest that had been soaked in tar and set alight.*

*6. Divorce Papers from an advocate's office.*

*7. Medicine labels.*

*8. A left shoe, size nine.*

*9. Five pages from a book. The pages were consecutive.*

*10. Three cardboard funnels painted yellow. Each was reduced to a fragile pile of ash. This ash was later glued to the interior glass of a vivarium.*

**Since burnt flying toys were now considered to be legitimate for inclusion, there were demands that other damaged toy items should be entertained as acceptable exhibits for a future toy exhibition.**

## [68] CATEGORY 25. SETTLING THE OLD FOR THE NEW.

**Here are some of the toys Izek Bable remembers owning, but which were probably originally thrown away because they were broken in some way.**

*1. A ball that rotated on a spindle that did not work and kept sticking.*

*2. A painted skittle with a scratch down one side.*

*3. A ripped fencing glove.*

*4. A torn paper hat.*

*5. A parchment mask that was constructed to be buckled around the mouth, but the buckle was missing. "I kept it because it belonged to my grandmother who nurtured very noisy grandchildren."*

*6. A wicker basket with a broken handle.*

*7. An almost entirely exhausted candle stuck with rusty pins.*

*8. A chair with a broken perforated seat.*

*9. An almost bald doll. Some evidence of use as a treasured toy was indicated by scratches on the bald head made perhaps by the small fingernails of children eager to eradicate the hair completely.*

*10. A screw of dirty crimson paper wrapped around with black cotton for sticking in your ear. It was one of a pair, but the other one, the one for the left ear, was missing.*

*11. A scraggy woolen doll made of straw and burnt brown paper. It was one of seven.*
*"I stood the children in a line, one for each doll, and demanded*

*to know why they kept their toys so regimented. My audience of seven small children fidgeted. They were intimidated." "They were being disrespectful," said Finister Croesus, a girl from the South, abandoned by her parents for being too noisy.*

**The toy that was the Jill-in-a-Box that laughed like a regal queen when you opened the lid was stolen. The likely thief was Opsinger Dedestry who enjoyed the female laughter which would have cheered any melancholy soul to joy indeed, especially someone as morose, disgruntled and tactiturn as he was. He had heard the laughter in the Wouverain dormitory when it was Eerio's turn to temporarily own the toy. The female voice was truly joyous. Unselfconsciously rich in irony, undoubtedly sexy. Eerio and Esquila had agreed for each to temporarily own the Jill-in-a-Box for a week at a time, since they had discovered it almost together, and realizing it was something very special and gave them so much joy. Opsinger Dedestry used his authority to visit the dormitory where Eerio kept a great many of his collected toys and he rummaged in that glass-case beside Eerio's bed and he had taken it.**
**Opsinger Dedestry was secretive and kept the Jill-in-a-Box in a leather sack slung over his shoulder and the sack never left him. Eerio and Esquila mourned the loss of the toy. They surprisingly at first did not discover that Opsinger had stolen it. They set traps to catch the thief not being certain who he, or indeed she, might be. They tracked it down eventually to a tar-covered shack in the Wouverain Mountains.**

**Eerio heard the Jill-in-a-Box laughter on a hilltop among the sheep and the goats on the Wouverain mountainside and finally discovered it was Opsinger Dedestry who was the thief. Eerio reported the theft to Lutumariner, and he had the Jill-in-a-Box wrestled from Opsinger Dedestry and taken to his office. Then Lutumariner mysteriously went into seclusion. He kept his office door locked and listened to that Jill-in-a-Box for days on end all on his own. The voice of that woman in the Jill-in-the Box was all too familiar to him.**

[70] CATEGORY 26. THE ATTRACTION OF THE DAMAGED

**Here are six more toys that appear to have been damaged in Izek Bable's remembrance.**

*1. A model soldier with yellow leggings. The model soldier used to belong to a cook and smelt of marzipan.*

*2. A nose from a stone statue of Pyramides the Scholar.*

*3. A snake skin you could animate with your fingers to pretend the snake was still alive, but sleepy.*

*4. An imitation loaf of bread made of plaster painted with replicas of currents and sultanas. It was gritty to the taste.*

*5. A patched hat of a figure of Winter. "Wet your hair thoroughly and put the hat on your head and you could hear the cold wind blow."*

*6. A miniature castle wall complete with slits for firing miniature thunder-bolts. Someone had widened the slits with a pencil.*

**The pastry-cook Izek Bable introduced the three orphan boys, the ginger-haired Eerio Padebourne, the blonde-haired Irium Bostero and the black-haired Jendro Hisloper, to his ten-year old nephew, Stoolie Gordon, who was not an orphan and lived with his father and stepmother in the tower-mill at Sisley. Visitors to Stoolie's house were in the habit of asking Stoolie who the adults in the room were, because they had difficulty understanding who or what parents actually were for, and what their purpose could be.**
**This Sisley tower-mill was one of the first towers erected to see the Hypothetical Sea, an idea that was slowly but steadily gaining some credence.**

CATEGORY 27. IMAGINING THE NEW DREAMS.

**Here are eight of the toys the pastry-cook's nephew, Stoolie Gordon, imagined he would have liked to have owned.**

*1. "I would have liked to have owned a baillie which is a sort of whistle that blows bubbles if you can get hold of any soap or grease or can find a toad and torment it and scrape its back to collect the soapy poison."*

*2 "A spy-glass to have ready by me when there might be an opportunity to see the sea. I kept it because I could never throw anything away."*

*3. A crayon "for drawing in the dark in order to show off."*

*4. "A bloodlothar that really works properly, which is very rare."*

*5. "A small model of a dog that would lick my hand and bite my enemies."*

*6. "A weather-vane that would tell me when the snow was about to come, and I could start oiling my sledge."*

*7."A cuscorn hat to wear when the South was talked about in school so that I could feel sympathy. My missing-believed-dead grandmother, who was my mother's mother, was from the South."*

*8. "A short toy dagger for pretending to kill my mother when she was angry with me for absolutely nothing at all. Then we could go shopping and she might buy me a red pencil so that I could make the blood really very red."*

CATEGORY 28. A NEW WORLD'S ANXIETIES.

**In association with Stoolie Gordon, more toys were found in the three primary classes of a poorly-funded orphanage in Hoffers Reach. It is said that many more of these particular**

[72] **toys were secreted there, and that Irium Bostero went back and rummaged for them.**

1. *Aester Feavour recalled that when she was three years old, she "had a doll with a wooden painted face and a body cut out of a flour sack and stuffed with acorns from the old tree in the paddock of the lame horse. The dry acorns became moist because of a long stay in a damp linen cupboard under the floorboards in the Large House. When the house was abandoned during "the Bad-Time Illness", the acorns sprouted and the doll became a forest called the Doll Forest. Then the doll died, I think."*

2. *A broken candle holder "dragged by a string that made a rattling sort of a noise, which if you were feeling unwell and a little scared, could sound like a metal ghost wearing clogs."*

3 *A dog-eared picture on paper of the Stoker of Lower Edge, "who we recognized because we had seen him often enough. He had a large white moustache, which he stroked with greasy fingers whilst eating pie. We watched him. And he gave me some pie and tickled me where my cousin Grundle said he shouldn't. But I think it was because Grundle wanted to tickle me in the same place."*

4. *A wooden standing-up figure of a tipcroft with a hat and painted gloves and a painted shadow. "The shadow was painted blue, which was strange because we had a good look at our shadows on the floor and they were not blue at all."*

5. *A speckled mirror. It had once been owned "by a brown-haired boy who had a squint in his left eye on account of being constipated. We think he was called Spammy Hedger and he lived in a bordello, which is a place you don't want to be living in, because they accuse you there for being lewd. Spammy Hedger stole the speckled mirror. He collected reflections. It was not a good idea for your reflection to get caught in Spammy Hedger's speckled mirror. Because if you were caught Spammy*

*Hedger could do things to you. Like change the colour of your hair, make you walk funny. Garble and confuse your speech. Add years to your last birthday. Even tell your mother, if you had a mother, you were not her child, which was a terrible thing to do."*

*6. A bezoar shaped like a crouching frog caught in an attitude of persistent hibernation, eyes closed, back arched, toes curled up. It was taken from the stomach of a cow who died in calf.*

*7. An anonymous turnip figure dressed in pieces of silver paper that always smelt of aniseed.*

*8. "A stuffed bird, originally perhaps a magpie, though its tail feathers were cut short, and we all know that magpies have long tail feathers. And it had only one red eye and it's only red-eyed pigeons that have red eyes. In both eyes, normally, that is."*

*9. A grandfather's black felt hat big enough for a small girl to sit in. Racheller who was six, took off all her clothes to amuse her brothers and squatted inside the hat and sang the Fillabee Song ten times. They stuck marbles in Racheller's ears and gave her an apple to stop her squealing. She fell asleep in the hat. Her grandfather found her, comforted her, though apparently she did not need comforting, took her to a Cookery to give her a bunterbread sandwich to cheer her up, found her brothers and beat them. Racheller's eldest brother reported the grandfather to the School Council and he was reprimanded for offering preferential treatment to females.*

*10. A torqued, scratched, over-boiled and charred wooden cooking spoon, chewed at the base of the handle by immature teeth.*

*11. A pair of spectacles without lenses "for seeing ants and spiders and other things close-up." She did not want to say anymore. She ran off crying.*

[74] *12. A small book whose pages had been bleached. Deciphering the almost totally obliterated text on the pages was a fascination that kept Harrie and Feckling and Ravestead Harvester quiet for hours on end so that their mother could make babies with men from the street.*

*13. A curl of brown hair tied with a piece of copper wire. The contrast between organic human hair which had once been alive, and inorganic metal which had always been nothing but dead, was always fascinating.*

*14. A grey wig belonging to Satquat's father. Satquat sat in it and it came down to his knees. It was like a coachman's winter cloak around him.*

*15. A small pretend boat made of bound yellow rushes. Toys as memories. "It reminded me of when I was six years old and refused to get out of the bath-water, even when it had grown so cold I turned blue and was shivering."*

*16. A stick for beating. Beating anything you like. Even your own buttocks. Which hurt.*

*17. An inside-out vest.*

*18. A flag. "It was cut from a blue bedspread that had formerly covered my grandmother's second-best bed. We used it to wave to the Marshal of Proctor when he walked by on Waving Day."*

*19. A snowball kept for forty days in cold storage. Rippler's father eventually used it to cool a glass of beer.*

*20. A broken heap. Three children sat in this heap day and night and could not be moved. They said that they were too comfortable to move.*

*21. A dead crow without maggots this time.*

*22. A small lunatic child kept in a dim light in a small room without a window. He had a knitted woollen hat pulled right down to his eye-brows. He did not react much to poking, but was regarded as a toy when his sisters were bored.*
*"I believe his name was Federico", said Rorario, his only friend, and she was certainly not very friendly.*

*23. A large see-through bottle-bag made from a pig's bladder that entertained Clever Pascoe for five days because he kept his tadpoles in it, but it killed his cousin Rachel because she emptied out the tadpoles and made the bag into a hat that slipped over her face and choked her. And she died.*

## CATEGORY 29. NEW MORALITIES AND NEW OWNERSHIPS.

**Fifteen toys that had new owners.**

**Fifteen toys were discovered by a family of orphans who had been encouraged to believe that finding a lost item could be construed as making the finder its legitimate new owner. This idea fashioned the opinions about toy ownership with Eerio Padebourne. As an orphan, he knew that his father had died in The Continental Troubles with "a punctured stomach", but it was rumoured that his grandfather was still alive. If you have lost your father but had a grandfather, did this mean you could claim to be an orphan? If it did, then, when challenged, Eerio Padebourne said that his grandfather gave him permission to remain the owner of the toys he had found and collected.**
**A formal listing or a more formal authoritative catalogue for the toys was developing. It was becoming a catalogue of ordered fragments, certainly obsessed with list-making where the lists almost seek to be more important than the connecting pieces of narrative and the speculation that apparently joined them together.**

**Confumo had started making elaborate notes and he was writing an introduction to a grand toy catalogue. In it, he**

[76] declared that toys, which in part are familiar and in part unfamiliar, are the product of children's imaginative play where practically everything available is turned into a play object. The scraps, detritus, rubbish and the discarded substance of everyday life are transfigured. What had one significance in adult life became something else to be reconsidered in a child's life. He considered that, for a great part of the time each"'home-grown» or remade or discovered or rediscovered toy object, was a representation of what was currently happening in the world. Thus a broken wheel could be considered a broken transport system to be remade A waving white handkerchief could be the evidence of a mass surrender and the end of all war. A shattered doll wearing a crown could be a toppled monarchy. A dead bird could be an image of destruction from the air.

Lutumariner thought that these ideas were far too grand. What would a child know about politics and current affairs? Few children could read. And even if they could read, what would they read? "These big ideas were too far from a child's experience." But he could agree that a toy's significance could often be understood in a different but equally powerful way, more complex, more complicated than what at first appeared most obvious. Many toys symbolically for a child recalled a devastating tragedy, or a great affection, or a great love, or a great loss, or indicate a great hope, a desire for escape, to sleep forever, to disappear or simply to die and be no more. These emotions were much closer to home, to recover from, for example, the disappearance of a loved one, the generosity of a stranger, sudden good fortune, or a sudden respite from pain.

*1. First, there was recovered a piece of string knotted at irregular intervals for various imaginative purposes,"perhaps to act as a telling-rope, though that's an adult idea, perhaps a whip, though that could be an adult idea too, a fishing line for fish without water or a washing-line ready to dry my underclothes if I were to have any, or as a counting device or a time-line to measure the days until I am twelve, and can have a baby, or be given a baby by a fish-wife, if I am considered to be good enough."*

*2. Second, it is supposed that there was recovered a much-damaged doll that sat on a throne on wheels. Eerio Padebourne is supposed to have said that it was his mother. This is unconfirmed. It is all supposition. He is supposed to have coveted this doll and said that it rightly belonged to him since he was an orphan and looking for his mother. He said it had been sent to him by his grandmother. This was not true. None of this is said to be true.*

*3. Third, "two sticks and a third stick to make a bird for my father to fly back home to my mother and me, his daughter by Elsie Faery, who is away just now."*

*4. A kite with a face like the moon. Some children say that the moon does not have a face but the markings really make the shape of a rabbit standing on its hind quarters.*

*5. Gum-sucks made of smelly grease. "They stick to your fingers." said Mercy Groose. "Like memories." said Vixey Pushover.."Though you can never tell if these are good memories or bad memories." Said Sandrey Fleece. These three under-weight small girls, all aged seven, were cousins. All three had broken thumbs, a heritage from their step-father who was blind.*

*6. "Rumple-sticks which is a game I have re-invented and which you can play under the blanket at night with a candle-end and three bags of twigs and a serviette ring if you are clever and you can make your ginney damp enough."*

*7. "Just another doll that I could give to my mother so that she could hug it very tight whilst we lay together on the stone flags under the apple tree in the yard. If she likes I could paint my cheeks red rosey and be the doll."*

*8. A small box for sending home to myself when I was away.*

*9. An alphabet book I was given so that I could tell the time.*

*10. "A blanket with roses on it, and a good sort of smell about it, but it can't be the roses, they are too grown up for me to appreciate, besides there are often thorns and the petals would droop and then fall off and we would have to sweep them off the back-stairs where I live. I think the good smell is of my mother who is lying just at this moment under the apple tree in the yard, drunk, or even dead. Or at least she could be playing dead."*

*11. "A doll that sits in a puddle of its own pee, a girl-doll. I could not want a boy doll because I wouldn't understand how a boy's pee works properly, my brother says. But of course he is wrong."*

*12. "And a farmer's glove for pulling lambs out of sheep which I put on my stump to pretend I am a two-handed farmer, or at least a two-handed farmer's wife, but I am only a girl with one hand. I hide my stump most of the time. Under the table or in my pocket, or under my blouse where I can sometimes rub my nipples with it to get them to become excited. Or bleed. Should I think of this glove as a toy? After all no one takes me seriously when I put the glove on. They say, leave her alone, she's still just a child and she only has one hand, just leave her alone."*

*13. Fourteen marbles, though fifteen would be nicer.*

*14. Just another doll that has two complete arms.*

**There were disputes about ownership among these orphans. There were fights and bruised foreheads.**

CATEGORY 30. SUDDEN DISTURBING OLD MEMORIES.

**Lutumariner had disappeared for two weeks. It was reported that he had gone to the country in the hills around Filistree where his mother had once owned a house. It was said that he had been upset for some reason by the Jill-in-a Box toy. It was said that the toy had alerted a strong personal memory.**

To re-establish himself as regards the post-war Toy Collection, Lutumariner declared anew that he was the master originator of The Historians Project. Nobody could disagree with that. It was he indeed who had felt irreducibly manoeuvred into the writing of a grand history of the new century to assuage some sort of guilt. It was considered that his grand history was to be some sort of compensation, a reparation. Looking back, this rediscovered Jill-in-a-Box toy, was a trigger. It was gradually understood that the optimistic female voice that was at the centre of its existence was the voice of the Matriarch Perpetua. His involvement with this woman explained a great deal. It was becoming obvious that he wanted to use the Toy Project as a way to make him part of the Investigation to release him from some assumed responsibility.

Lutumariner, shocked into remembering his past, eventually came out of self-instigated isolation. It was surely he who now allocated suitable funding to Opsinger Dedestry, the Director of the Wouverain Orphanage, and indirectly to his three charges, the ginger-haired Eerio Padebourne, the blonde-haired Irium Bostero and the black-haired Jendro Hisloper. Thanks to Lutumariner's authority the Toy Project received official sanction. On the strength of the new funding, Opsinger Dedestry employed a secretary whose name was Loadstar Fives.

Within a month it was suggested, relevant to its new funding and consequent respectability, that the toy archivists should move away from orphanages and address their attentions to more official educational establishments for children. It was a salient fact that orphanages reminded the establishment of strife and failure. Children without parents were a black mark on the recovery from the Continental Troubles.

Stoolie Gordon, the nephew of the pastry-cook Izek Bable could be a guide to more optimistic establishment futures. Unlike the ginger-haired Eerio Padebourne, the blonde-haired Irium Bostero, and the black-haired Jendro Hisloper, Stoolie Gordon had parents. He introduced the three orphan boys to

[80] **the Oratory School at Wouverain where a pupil's imagination was to be encouraged in the service of legal advocacy. Here is a short list of toys compiled by Stoolie Gordon.**

CATEGORY 31. NEW POSSIBILITIES FOR IMPROVEMENT.

*1. A parchment funnel used to increase the volume of a human voice in oratorical auditions. A small boy called Preacher stood in a tunnel under the Mocker Highway to practice with it. He read out the Pigment Salaries and the Opportunity Practices, and recited the Seventy Articles of the Flossery, and started on the Edicts of the Sanctimony but became frightened at the gravity of some of the Summonses and stopped as the echoes got louder, and he ran out of the tunnel and fell into the river Pessatus and was swept away down towards the Woodenfall Weir and was never seen again.*

*2. Four thick books glued together to make a podium for an ambitious scholar to increase his height when engaged in public speaking.*

*3. A toy umbrella with twined snakes for a handle. It had probably been owned by the small sister of a young advocate who refused to get his hair wet.*

CATEGORY 32. KEEPING ALIVE PERSONAL MEMORIES.

**A toy introduced by Izek Bable in response to a sudden personal memory. Personal memories were becoming significant.**

**This personal memory was at one time considered prophetic as regards future accusations of moral infamy aimed in Izek Bable's direction.**

*1. A wooden head of a lawyer much rubbed by curious enquiring fingers. The head had a wig. It had eyes made of pieces of blue glass. The figure was regarded sometimes as a female. Perhaps it was a portrait. And it sat upright in a box. The box was seen as a primitive throne.*

## CATEGORY 33. INTRODUCING NEW POSSIBILITIES.

### Toys from the Espionage School at Wouverain. This is a list compiled by Stoolie Gordon and Irium Bostero

*1. A small box painted red inside and black outside waiting to be filled with evidence. What could that evidence be? Small dead fish? Sticklebacks and minnows? Damaged butterflies? Meadow-browns? Brimstones? Cabbage-whites? White mice with pink eyes? Corks from fizzy wine bottles? Small chequered skirts?*

*2. A pot of opaque glass containing a liquid that smelt of turpentine.*

*3. A leather bag containing dried peas, each one numbered in white paint applied with a very small squirrel-haired paintbrush. There appeared to be no continuity in the numbers. Combinations of numbers in twos, threes, eights or thirteens for example, seemed to have no significance. Perhaps only the first owner of the leather bag knew exactly what the significance of the numbers intended.*

*4. A glass globe with a cork stopper containing three human cauls, rare evidence, it is said, of an infamous birth. They seemed to have no value at all. Many children wanted to see these "envelopes" for small babies. They wanted to be born wearing a helmet. The children wanted to hold them, touch them, even stretch them over their own heads like a head-*

*hugging swimming cap. And wonder why they themselves had not possessed a caul when they had emerged from their mother's belly. But perhaps they had and that their mothers had thrown them away, believing them perhaps to be unlucky. The children asked whether boys were more likely to have possessed cauls than girls? They asked if it was true that girls with cauls should always spell their names with capital letters. They asked if it was true that children born with cauls would have special futures playing ball, swimming in warm water, changing sex, being good at mathematics? It is known that certain poets were born wearing a caul, born with a bonnet indeed, born indeed as a helmet-headed baby. A caul was prized by sailors who would pay a considerable price for such a rarity when it was known that those born with a caul would never drown.*

*5. A small wooden box stained inside with cherry sauce. If you placed your nose close to the lid of the box you could smell cherries. And you could be encouraged to see fields of pink cherry blossom stretching to the horizon. And you could have before you a white porcelain bowl of cherries without stones.*

*6. A metal flask that at one time had contained plum brandy to sustain timorous witnesses at a show-trial.*

*7. A stained white envelope containing a crown drawn with a pen and ink on a sliver of brown wrapping paper. These items were in demand by children who did not possess shoes.*

*8. A small wooden box with six compartments for pins, needles, cotton-thread, croquet-hooks, thimbles and ribbons. It had a blood stain on the inside of its lid, probably from a pricked finger belonging to a young seamstress. "Aspiring to melodrama," it said on the door of this diminutive sewing cupboard.*

*9. A bag containing a single acorn.*

*10. A cardbox box containing a green beetle with missing legs and missing antennae.*

*11. A metal phial containing a child's desiccated thumb, "All that was left of my brother Alfro after the attack of the bears." Said Tillering. She was not completely telling the whole truth. She also had Alfro's tongue.*

*12. A hollow space in a small book containing a buckle heavily corroded with verdigris.*

*13. A dead cat. "I could not part with it. If I did it would mean like losing my childhood all over again."*

*14. A twist of paper containing twenty tines from a bone comb and a few human hairs.*

*15. A hollow memory-stick notched for dates. The dates were indecipherable.*

*16. A momento which was a bad-debt note stuck through with a rusty needle, "from a place called Morsch which is a great way off, and where Pallow's ugly paternal grandmother lived because of the Meeting of the Widows after the Stirrup Campaign. His other grandmother, the beautiful one, lived in PastonCumber. Pallow favoured his ugly grandmother."*

*17. A plate for collecting charity coins along with a selection of shirt buttons and a green mottled marble.*

*18. A small box called a"conventilator".*

*19. A leather bag full of almonds for horses. Horses favour almonds that have been salted.*

*20. A toy horse made of candle spliffs.*

**The three orphans, the ginger-haired Eerio Padebourne, the blonde-haired Irium Bostero and the black-haired Jendro Hisloper, were growing older. Eerio Padebourne could now be**

[84] twelve, Irium Bostero was possibly eleven, and Jendro Hisloper could have been as old as thirteen.

There is a saying that declared *"When I was a child, I spoke as a child, I understood as a child, I thought as a child: but when I became a man, I put away childish things."* We should not necessarily believe this to be so indelibly true. The child lives long inside the adult and perhaps never dies.

Some changes in attitude towards the boys' fascination with toys did become noticeable in the formation of the Toy Collection. "Boys with toys" became in some spheres, a derogatory insult. But the same original ambitions did hold sway and the original concerns continued to be pursued. The changes will gradually be realized. For example, there had been a stigma associated with the project because of its connection to orphanages. That stigma was fading as the difference between being an orphan and being a child connected to a blood-related family was disappearing. The personal interest of Lutumariner in the toy project was noticed and Opsinger Dedestry's self-advertising habits were creating an effect. Various interest groups eager to see a future in the swell of interest to find practical ways and means to further the welfare of children took note. A movement to concentrate on the mother and child relationship was growing. The position of the female was re-authorised. And the dignity of the Wouverain Sorority increased.

A search began through attics and cellars and outhouses in war-ransacked domestic buildings. It was seriously considered that abandoned or semi-abandoned collections of children's toys might possibly be discovered. And there was a greater sympathy for the very young.

To find material to pass over to the newly stimulated foundation Isek Bable became a focus for collecting materials. His former solidarity with the army in the PastonCumber region became significant.

## CATEGORY 34. NEW POSSIBILITIES FOR THE VERY YOUNG WHO MUST BE COSSETTED.

**A list of toys for very young children. This list was compiled by Trusty Completer, a cousin of Jendro Hisloper, after he had become an orphan when his parents died in an accident involving a runaway racing horse called Umbrellophon.**

*1. A teething ring made of bone attached to a bell.*

*2. An amulet made of petrified resin.*

*3. An ivory bangle, needle-burnt at intervals along its length that indicated the events of a private history. It was attached to a red rattle of dried beans.*

*4. A head band sewn with red glass beads and slices of mirror.*

*5. A wooden, animated, articulated snake that hissed when it was pulled along the ground by means of a red cord.*

*6. A bell with a tassel.*

*7. A bell with two tassels.*

*8. A rattle filled with dried peas.*

## CATEGORY 35. DEVICES TO ENCOURAGE IMAGINATION.

**The Historian Lutumariner had been unsettled by the finding of the Jill-in a Box Toy. Often he was now up at dawn, saddled and breakfasted before seven o'clock, taking his small black pony Saddlemass along with wife Daisirai, and had arrived at Allchanging on the Richtag Ridge some five miles south of the foothills of the Wouverain Mountains where there was small hostelry. Here he settled in a rattan chair with a bowl of**

[86] oatmeal fritters and cream and stared at the distant blue hills of the Wouverain Mountains, talking to his wife about newly born children, serial adultery, abortions, infidelity, desertion and orphans of the war. Daisirai, having heard it all before, nodded and knitted. It was a conversation that was, she knew therapeutic and useful to set the old Historian's troubled mind at ease. Lutumariner, she knew, was thinking of Perpetua. The Matriarch. His eyes were still focused on the blue hills. Occasionally a stately woman with big breasts, wide hips and heavy feet, walked the dusty road in front of the hostelry, bid Lutumariner and his wife a nod of recognition and walked on by. With a sigh, Lutumariner, got up, wiped his white whiskers, poured the rest of his fritters and cream on the grass verge for the quarrelsome magpies, got on his pony, his wife up behind him, and rode back to his house in Greasley for a day's History writing. The walls of his study were papered with Wouverain Mountain maps, featuring his scribbled memories of rail-tracks for go-carts. Junctions, turntables, points, viaducts, tunnels, sidings and side-rails all for whipping about the mountains.

Prompted by finding a black steeple hat in a sheep pen, Eerio Padebourne thought it could be wise to learn to become a magician. He sought out toys that might be of assistance. He collected all the usual apparatus like red paper noses, white rabbits, a black cloak with strings, a full-length double mirror, hot water that steamed, high-heeled red shoes, confetti and artificial flowers, playing cards, and a wire monkey that climbed a stick. And he read and digested all the relevant existing manuals and tried to remember all the instructions.

*1. The Southern Cross Trick.*
*"Keep an eye On the Southern Sky."*

*2. The Baker's Bun Trick.*
*"Use half a pint of baking soda to make the buns rise."*

*3. The Toad in the Hole Trick.*
*"Don't wait for the spawning season, catch the amphibians when they came out of their winter hibernation."*

*4. The Cross-Wires Trick.*
*"Use copper wire."*

*5. Cascardi's Trick.*
*"Make sure you pay Cascardi's widow. Otherwise it simply won't work."*

*6. The Unhappy Soldier Trick.*
*"Tell the soldier he can marry the widow."*

*7. The Bandaged Finger Trick.*
*"Just Pretend your index finger is broken."*

*8. he Sunstroke Puzzle.*
*"You cannot wait until the sun shines."*

*9. The Emperor's Ant Trick.*
*"Build a nest of evergreen leaves and paralyze the insects that way."*

*10. The Snake Surpise Trick.*
*"Banned in old people's homes because of unreasonable fear. Get the old people drunk and comatose on cherry brandy."*

*11. The Effervescent Wheel Trick.*
*"Use damp fireworks."*

*12. The Divorce Correspondent's Trick.*
*"Just go and kiss the plaintiff to demonstrate your sympathy."*

## CATEGORY 36. NEW MATERIALS TO BE EMBRACED.

**Toys made of metal. A list complied by Irium Bostero. There was a search to widen the substance of the toy collection in**

[88] **content and in materials. "If we wish to make this toy collection representative of the end of the War Years we must be more ambitious. It was afterall, metal swords, metal daggers, maces, axes, arrows-heads, lances, pistols, muskets, arquebuses, that enabled the winners to become the winners."**

*1. A tin pot with a spout once used in oiling the hinges of armour, now used for a doll's tea-party, pouring pretend hot water and pretend scarce milk.*

*2. A brass feruled sceptre demoted from some ceremonial purpose to be a small whip handle for urging on reluctant toy horses. The toy to be used with appropriate noises like "Jirrup", "Getupp", "Hurrah", "Hossay" and "Ride On".*

*3. A heavy metal disc of unknown origin, perhaps from the armature of a stand for supporting part of a human skeleton, the upper part, now useful as a throwing discus.*

*4. Two tin buttons wrapped in white cotton cloth which bore stains of rust. The buttons were tied together with a twist of copper wire.*

*5. A metal letter L, once used to help form the word* HELPING-HAND. *The other letters had been lost in an earthquake.*

*6. A metal hat with a red-painted brim, jointed with six symmetrically spaced small brass bolts. The front brim tipped up when the eyes were not to be shaded.*

*7. A metal tube with a diameter of a quarter of an inch. Former purpose unknown. Present purpose could possibly be as a pea-shooter.*

*8. A disused paint-can fashioned from tin that had been pierced with holes to make a colander for straining blood from bandages, now utilised for draining sticklebacks out of pond water. It looked as though the paint-can had contained cream paint, then dark green paint and then cream paint again.*

*9. A funnel with serrated tines now used as a hat for naughty children in a game of Cropping the Dunce.*

*10. Two soup spoons welded back to back by an incompetent welder for making a doll.*

*11. A painted cut-out metal figure from a squire's helmet resembling a troubled bird, now a child's weather vane atop a barn roof.*

*12. The metal clapper of a bell brought down by high winds, now used as a hammer in a nursery.*

*13. A pair of scissors with overlarge handles once owned by a seamstress who was a man, now bound about with red and yellow twine to represent the figure of the Scottage who had run amok in the Second Wolverain War, killing the Yellow Queen.*

*14. A hanger for petticoats made of chains and wire formerly scavenged from an arrow basket.*

*15. A metal bird which was a companion to a live canary in a gilded cage. The live canary ceased singing when the metal bird was taken away.*

*16. Seven pierced military medals strung on a string hung around the neck of seven-year old Lucy Smalls.*

*17. A lump of ambiguous metal which could have been identified as the left-over from a mould associated with the manufacture of a sword guard.*

*18. Two metal handles to a small cannon used to grip a rope for skipping purposes.*

*19. A buckle fashioned with a pair of wings now a brooch.*

*20. A metal cap fashioned to protect a newly-sharpened pencil.*

*21. A right-hand shoe fashioned from stamped tin that had been corroded in some mild acid and looked now as though it had been fashioned from the yellow spotted leather from the belly of some unidentifiable reptile from the South.*

*22. A square of metal, maybe tin, cut at one time from a section of a bowl or a ewer, that bore a painted representation of the Sea fashioned with black curls on turquoise that suggested pubic hair on the blue belly of a fat man.*

## WATER

**Then Opsinger Dedestry, the director of the Wouverain Orphanage, lost his wife in a boating accident in winter fog. He became melancholy, though there was some suspicion that his emotional distress was faked and that Dedestry was in some way responsible for his wife's death. To distract himself from the memory of his loss, or pretend loss, and also perhaps from the constant prying interviews of the water-bailiffs who were responsible for that particular stretch of the river where Dedestry's wife had drowned, he began to immerse himself more deeply in the children's toy project. Then there was a rumour that Dedestry's wife had committed suicide. Opsinger Dedestry encouraged Irium Bostero to spend considerable amounts of time with communities of river-folk. Some said it was to distract attention from his own problems with water, of drowning, and of his wife's death.**

**The opposition of views about the sea of Opsinger Dedestry on the one hand and the pastry-cook Izek Bable on the other, became well known and universally recognized. Opsinger Dedestry denied there could be anything that resembled a sea. Izek Bable was convinced that a sea was a possible idea and that a sea should be searched for.**

CATEGORY 37. FUTURES.

**Opsinger Dedestry said that Toys associated with water could be considered as exercises in ephemerality, water being so fluid and changeable, spending so much of its time as ice or steam or clouds. Or tears. He compiled a list of so-called water-toys. It did not go unremarked of course that water had been the apparent cause of his wife's unexpected death.**

*1. A shifter.*

*2. A glass jar for filling and emptying blue water.*

*3. A paperboat marked with the colours of the Shine.*

*4. A decoy duck made of wood, painted, and ballasted with lead pellets to make it float evenly and upright.*

*5. A miniature watermill wheel with the spindle intact made for a model of hydraulics.*

*6 A cup with a hole in the base for tricking people.*

*7. A cracked saucer with a lid for floating beans in water to make them swell.*

*8. A two-coloured water-flay for a river-boat.*

*9. A long log with an inserted metal keel.*

*10. A water butterfly.*

*11. A painted wooden fish-lure, light blue on the underside to be disguised against the sky, dark blue from above to contrast with deep water. It was hung above a baby's cot.*

*12. A tray used to float on water.*

*13. A model of the sea. All blue and white dashes.*

*14. A cup with a small hole drilled in its base. The size of the hole was determined by a calculation which would let out the water in the filled cup in exactly one minute.*

*15. A metal breast that could be filled with water if milk was unavailable.*

*16. A ceramic life-sized head with large ears which was used as a watering-can.*

*17. Seven dyes to pour over a waterfall to change the colour of the water to mimic the colours of the rainbow.*

*18. A mirror that cast a blue reflection.*

*19. Two metal cans connected with a metal pipe of small bore. Tipping the water from one can to the other produced the sound of water running in a deep underground chamber.*

**Water became a subject on everyone's mind. The current understanding of water and the mythical sea suppposedly centred in the far South. The mountains in the North where The Wouverain Hills were dominant, persuaded the rain-clouds to climb high in the air and release their load of water. This water-load accumulated and fell as heavy rain into three valleys creating three rivers which swelled into raging torrents called the Fovant, the Basset and the Voluntary. The Fovant rushed directly Southwards to the west of PastonCumber, the Voluntary flowed almost Southwards to the east of PastonCumber, and the Basset flowed with some irregularity right through the centre of PastonCumber.**
**Then the three wide rivers flowed rapidly southwards in approximate parallel trajectories for five hundred miles to the Southern border to arid country which various peoples called "unattractive scrub" and then a further five hundred miles to where people called the country "uninhabitable desert" and**

then a further five hundred miles they described as "exhausting aridity" into hundred of hundreds of miles of yellow sand to reappear or be reborn in "aquifers" possibly for a thousand miles further south to create the Southern Seas.

Many people believed this and many people did not. Those that did believe it thought of these Southern Seas as Paradise or Heaven. Many people simply did not believe any of it and were convinced that the waters that were supposed to flow as aquifers simply did not exist and that the mighty deserts were hundreds of miles deep and simply dried up all the water or else led it so deep into the earth, it must have ended up on the other side of the planet.

Opsinger did not believe in this Heavenly place. Lutmariner did. Bable did believe in it and convinced Eerio who already had begun to believe it because Fontenay did.

CATEGORY 38. ANXIETIES FOR THE FUTURE.

Toys that have caused injury and death. This list was compiled by Opsinger Dedestry when he spent six days in a waterside lock-up accused of his wife's death. The rumour of his wife's possible suicide was now complicated by an accusation that it was brought about by jealousy of her husband's seduction of a young woman on her sixteenth birthday. This boatman's daughter was associated with the Wouverain Matriarchy. Opsinger Dedestry was starting to become a threat to young women. He was cautioned. Provocatively he compiled a list for the toy directory. Counter-provocatively Eerio made it his business to turn the list into real objects that could indeed be seen as toys.

> *1. Painted plugs for the mouth and the nostrils and other entrances employed to prevent the water from entering the human body.*

*2. A wooden doll painted to imagine the doll was in the throes of having a baby.*

*3. A ladder painted green with poorly made joints between the verticals and the third, fourth, seventh and ninth rungs.*

*4. Crutches for making landscape progress with the minimum use of the legs.*

*5. Poles for jumping and leaping.*

*6. A mannikin for submersing, to determine its probabilities of drowning if it had no limbs.*

**Opsinger Dedestry's list could be regarded as being spiteful and mean-spirited.**

## CATEGORY 39. LOOKING TO WATER TO SETTLE ANXIETIES FOR THE FUTURE.

**Here are six toys caught by a trawling net and a fishhook by Clement Frookle and his sister Scatter, acquaintances of Irium Bostero. They were much taken by Bostero's easy smile and his great charm. They made a hoard of toys in the backyard of their wooden house on the river-quay at Shorts. They were eager to support the idea of a Grand Exhibition of Toys.**

**Toys fished from the river by Clement Frookle and his sister Scatter.**

*1. A wicker basket to be held above the water-line by floats.*

*2. A rope attached to a float shaped like a turtle.*

*3. A cork saucer.*

*4. A doll with a swim bladder.*

*5. A stoppered bottle with a weighted base and a tin flag.*

*6. A toy boat made from reeds bound with string.*

**The following toys had been caught by a hooked wire anchor by Asprey Docking and his mother. They made a hoard on a barrow in the fish-shed in their garden.**

*1. A bundle of pins stuck in a velvet cushion much diminished by being in water.*

*2. An irridiscent ballbearing to be run up and down a lead guttering.*

*3. A glass doll's eye with a metal pin stuck in its iris.*

*4. An empty metal box shaped like a fiddle.*

*5. Three cogs on a metal wire.*

*6. A key-ring with a bakery bolt.*

*7. A wedding ring thrown away.*

*8. A shoe with a silver heel once worn by an unhappy bride.*

**These toys, all having metal associations, had been caught by a large magnet and small winch by the three Botherly Brothers and their idiot father. The father gibbered and wet his underwear, but his sons refused prestigious jobs with money-lenders to succour him. The four of them were deliriously happy and sang all day.**

*9. A cart with metal axles.*

*10. A work-horse halter complete with a horse skeleton.*

*11. A fire bucket full of metal fish.*

[96] **Irium Bostero observed the habits of small children living along the banks of the three big rivers, the Astrict, the Flowing and the Slow Madder, watching their immature attempts to reconstruct certain aspects of the world and its civilization in miniature with basic materials such as river-beached sand, gravel, soil and mud. They were finding out for themselves through play the rudimentary characteristics of gravity, plasticity and durability. They ingeniously used what was to hand as play tools. Children along the banks of all three rivers appeared to be fascinated by building towers.**

CATEGORY 40. PREPARING TO BUILD FOR A NEW FUTURE.

**Six toy-tools for playing in sand and fine gravel to build miniature castles, roads, bridges and towers. It was interesting that so many of these particular toys seemed to have started their life in a kitchen.**

*1. A section of metal, perhaps an alloy of iron and tin, with a triangular cross-section that might at one time have been a section of a metal picture framing. It was variously used for marking wet sand banks with an over-lapping V-shaped texture to suggest grass, or for furrowing miniature fields or for dragging in wet mud to make miniature rivers.*

*2. A serrated object that could once have been a carpenter's rasp, one time fixed in a wooden handle that was now absent, presumed lost. It was frequently used in the making of castellations.*

*3. A short wooden brush support that no longer held bristles, though the drilled holes that had once supported the bristles were still in evidence, even if filled in with an accumulation of soil and small stones. It was useful for patting sand hard to make a secure base for building castles of sand and mud. When used forcefully enough, the indentations made by the absent bristle holes could be made visible.*

*4. A rusted fish-frying implement with twenty-one holes arranged in a pattern of three times seven. This was used also for patting mud and sand hard and for making regular patterned textures.*

*5. A metal whisk with broken tines. If scrambled in wet sand it could be used to make a texture that stood in for tangled vegetation, a forested hillside, a stormy sea, the frizzled hair of a man on fire, a snow-storm or the fur of a river rat.*

*6. A bone which might have been the femur of a small dog. It had been broken at one end and sanded and rubbed sufficiently, no doubt over a period of some time, to form a sharp chiselled end suitable for dragging in wet sand to make miniature roads.*

## CATEGORY 41. PREPARING FOR A NEW FUTURE WITH NEW TOOLS.

**Five tools found abandoned on the River Userell beach at Standing Straight when the local children ran down to the water's edge to watch Jursey Cuspa drown after suffering an attack of epilepsy.**
**The River Userell was a tributary of the Slow Madder. The tools had been used for shovelling mud to make buildings, animals, roads, tunnels, castle, towers and fanciful decorations on the back of an imaginary sea monster.**
**Some observers said later that Jursey Cuspa had not drowned but had choked on a grossly swollen tongue enlarged because he told too many lies.**

*1. A metal spoon with a broken handle that could be used for scratching, scooping and ladling small amounts of water.*

*2. A wooden stick with a splintered end that could be used to perform the services of a brush.*

*3. Half a delicate decorated china cup, broken such that the handle could still be employed to hold the damaged bowl and use it as a shovel. Small pink flowers and a gold coloured rim made children feel they were playing with a queen's birthday present, broken by a clumsy servant and thrown in sorrow into the back of a kitchen midden.*

*4. A dibbler, sometims called a pusher in the nursery as in "spoon and pusher" being implements to accustom a small child to use adult utensils at the dining-table.*

*5. A large brass key with a twisted operational end which had probably been twisted because the shaft of the key had been banged hard sideways whilst the head had been fixed in the lock.*

CATEGORY 42. A HOPEFUL NEW FUTURE IN A WORLD OF TOWERS.

## Seven things for fashioning miniature towers in miniature landscapes in a soil of wet sand and rotted plant fibre.

*1. A comb with twenty-five missing tines. It was evident that the metal comb had originally possessed two hundred tines. The metal had oxidised and was now coloured in a sepia-brown and a dark blue. Eight of the tines were coagulated with a once sticky substance, identity unknown; suggestions included honey, tar, pine-resin, even blood.*

*2. Unidentified object believed to have originated in a vinery. It was fashioned from bone, maybe even ivory, and was considered at one time to have been valuable.*

*3. A pen which at one time had been fashioned from a wing feather of a swan. The hollow-quill had been filled with molten lead. Since its fragility was recognised even by small children, it was used sparingly.*

*4. A table fork with two of its four tines missing. The flattened end of the handle was stamped with three raised dots in a triangular formation.*

*5. A knobknobbery made of a tree root studied with nails making an irregular texture when trailed through wet mud.*

*6. A dye-stop from a sunken ship owned by a consortium of drapers.*

*7. A calico printer's dye depicting a cow dipping its head to drink.*

## CATEGORY 43. PREPARING YET MORE MATERIAL FOR A HOPEFUL NEW FUTURE.

**Toys owned by the child Alizarin Gorightly, a boatman's daughter who lived above the banks of the Scullery, a tributary of the Slow Madder. She had lost her father in a river storm and had become an orphan, which was how she met Eerio Padebourne. There was always a recognized tendency, it was thought, that orphans congregated together, recognizing one another from afar. Was it a body posture, or a tone of voice, a certain reticence, an over-anxious desire to please, a predisposition to weep when treated generously? It was difficult to agree upon a set of characteristics.**

*1. A miniature practice sail with tags and ropes, ties and pulleys. It was accompanied with a small tin-whistle for issuing orders in code amongst river traffic.*

*2. A blue flag for matching a comparison with the colour of the sky, sometimes used as a meteorological aid.*

*3. A painted eye for watching for the wind.*

[100] *4. A pair of rope sandals for walking on the water.*

*5. A length of rope exactly forty metres long, the length of the great boat Goenard intended to launch on the sea when Bastinado found it.*

*6. A rowlock lacquered and burnished in fishmeal oil.*

*7. A pile of sand containing one hundred jet-black freshwater mussel shells.*

*8. A plaited reed posy for blessing floating babies.*

*9. A stuffed female fish painted yellow like the sun.*

*10. A plug of lead taken, it was said, from the bottom of the River Davitt where, by repute, warm water welled up from hot springs.*

*11. An apparatus for making a fountain.*

*12. An apparatus for making steam.*

*13. Artificial ripples.*

*14. A tattoo on pig-skin whose outline had once been popular with sailors. It had been copied from a marine painting.*

*15. A jammer.*

*16. A hypothetical marine map printed in blue squares, each square getting darker towards the bottom of the map to indicate perhaps the increasing cold temperature of the water, or perhaps the water's depth.*

*17. A spy-glass.*

*18. A noose to catch small whales.*

*19. A fishing net shaped in such a fashion as to be able to catch a giant freshwater octopus.*

*20. A miniature anchor made of incorruptible brass.*

**Eerio Padebourne now had six categories of water-associated toys which he thought ought to be displayed in appropriate settings when the exhibition rooms would be arranged. To assist him Irium Bostero made illustrations on white paper coloured with deep blue watercolour paint streaked with green patches. Perhaps influenced by the conversations he had with Izek Bable the pastry-maker, Eerio Padebourne was becoming interested in the idea of the hypothetical sea. Finding sheets of deep blue crumpled painted sandpaper in the carpenter's shed where Izek Bable constructed his sight-screens, he sought out other possible items that could be placed under the category of the hypothesized sea. Eerio persuaded Irium to consider making illustrations of how the future exhibition of toys should look like.**

## CATEGORY 44. THE IDEA OF THE POSSIBILITY OF A SEA.

*1. Glass from a warehouse splintered by pressure, an indication of the imagined power of the hypothetical sea.*

*2. A shallow baking tray rusted in parts by being left out in the rain. The rust is orange-yellow and represents the beaches around the perimeter of the hypothetical sea.*

*3. Spindles from the kitchen used in frying pieces of meat at orphanage festivals.*

*4. A large bed-sheet with various rips and tears splashed with blue dye and stretched on a washing line.*

[102] CATEGORY 45. IN EXPECTATION OF FINDING A SEA.

**Toys associated with dressing up. In association with people who might be interested in a hypothetical sea.**

*1. Red leather boots, a peeled branch and a pail. For dressing up as a sailor and stamping in the mud, whilst holding a peeled branch to represent a pike. The pail, placed upside down on the head, was worn as a helmet.*

*2. A pillow. For dressing up as a fat man, strutting with the pillow of feathers strapped to the belly with a crimson strap. Fat men were prized amongst sailors in the cold seas of the North. The excess flesh could often be a life-saver.*

*3. A sack. For dressing up as a water tramp, sometimes known as a beachcomber.*

*4. A sack. For dressing up as a bear.*

*5. A string of beads and a coloured belt. And nothing else.*

*6. Dressing up to look undressed.*

**Opsinger Dedestry's wife, Propellora, had been found dead on a sandbank of the Upper Slow Madder River. It was reported that Propellora's tongue was swollen so that it could not be poked back into her mouth.**

## CENSURESHIP & CONFISCATION

**An approximate count of the toys so far collected easily reached over the thousand mark. The foundations and funding bodies of the PastonCumber neighbourhood were**

**becoming interested in the Toys Project. It was rumoured that they were becoming jealous of its ability to attract publicity and funds. Many of them initiated projects to curb the current successes of the Toys Project. There were confiscations and censorships of toys. Eerie Padebourne insisted on putting them in a special category to register his objections to any form of toy censorship. Some confiscations and censorships were undoubtedly ephemeral and local, some were certainly the result of officious policy, but some perhaps were brought about by direct envy and rivalry.**

CATEGORY 46. THE NEW CENSORSHIP.

**It seemed that Dedestry was responsible for much of the new censorship.**
**Some of the confiscations can only be accounted for by their unfocussed eccentricity. Eight were certainly inspired by a desire to arrange still-lifes to please a particular subjective aesthetic sensibility which may have been Hisloper's.**

*1. A white-painted cone representing a mountain covered in snow, placed between a pile of newly polished brass coins and a fawn-coloured book of simple geometry.*

*2. A crimson wooden ball standing on a yellow book of mathematics.*

*3. A green-painted forked stick once used as a catapult, found leaning against a wooden pyramid that was sometimes used to illustrate geometrical perfection.*

*4. A figure of a farmer's wife made in papier mache that stood beside a broken white china-cup that was stained inside with honey.*

*5. A wooden black box containing porcelain balls for a game of Tripple, that stood between a roll of blue-squared graph paper and a stained clay pipe.*

*6. A miniature red wooden ladder leaning against a green-painted metal candle-stick.*

*7. A white-painted doll house stuffed with chopped straw that fell out of its three windows and pushed out of its three doors.*

*8. A geometrically-fashioned model tree made of plywood and decorated with hanging silver bells and painted a deep green that stood between a rock of volcanic origin, maybe it was even a meteorite, and a large, water-eroded smooth pebble, both wrapped around with string. There was a hand-written label on the rock which said "Earth" and a hand-written label on the pebble which said "Sea".*

CATEGORY 47. THE NEW CENSORSHIP CONTINUES.

**More confiscated Toys were discovered in the ashes of a bonfire in a schoolyard.**

*1. A partially burnt wooden disc with a serrated edge, believed to be associated with a throwing function.*

*2. A burnt wooden disc fitted with a square central hole, believed to be associated with a throwing function.*

*3. A wooden disc, so burnt as to represent a damaged new moon.*

*4. A partially burnt box of coloured chalks, each chalk fixed into a holder for easier handling.*

*5. A metal abacus with seventeen burnt beads.*

*6. A partially burnt flail decorated with brass nails.*

*7. A wooden doll, one metre high, with articulated arms and legs, with certain accentuated sexual characteristics and wearing a partially burnt broad-brimmed hat.*

**Poppae Stilts, a PastonCumber Historian, working on a history of containers, was interested in the contents of the pockets of children. She believed if uncontrived and unprepared and approached spontaneously and without warning, what children carried in their pockets was an indication of current social trends and activities, and on a wider level, could be construed as a trenchant comment about society in general. For example, carrying keys and small change was a comment on property and money, though very few children whose pockets Poppae Stilts ransacked had either keys or small change. Carrying pieces of stale food, bread-crusts and apple-cores was a comment on the fear of unassuaged hunger. Carrying an excess of matches, many of them spent, and kept and coveted in a belief that they could be reused, was relevant to an anticipated fear of the cold.**

**Poppae Stilts came to the Book Depository Store with three hundred paper bags each containing the contents of a child's pockets. Each paper bag was identified with the name and age of the owner of the pocket and sometimes with an approximate description of the child whose pockets had been picked. Here are descriptions of the lists of twenty-seven of those three hundred paper bags. Poppae was confronted often with unco-operative children. She listed their unco-operation in five ways. One. No name. Two. Un-named. Three. Mute. Four. Too shy to say a name. Five. Adamantly refused to say a name.**

*1. A ten-year old female – Martrap Begotal. Daughter of a miner. She had a blackened face and blackened hands.*
*In her pockets were a brass key, a pierced stone, a ten-inch length of brown string, a twist of paper that once may have held*

*a sweet called a Filbert, and a small denomination coin common in the South. Martrap Begotal was reluctant to talk and ran away to urinate noisily in a lead bucket to disparage those who had had the audacity to infringe her privacy.*

*2. A six-year old boy. Orphan. Red hair. Father killed in an explosion. In his pockets were an acorn, seven almonds, and a nose-rag cut from his sister's petticoat.*

*3. No name. A boy probably aged eight. No thumb on his left hand. He said it had been bitten off. No further explanation was offered. In his pockets were an apple-core, an almond for the prevention of toothache, a buckle, a river-washed pebble, a crumpled dock leaf associated with neutralizing nettle-stings, and an ambiguous object made of metal that could not be identified, but it was believed to be associated with ferrets.*

*4. An eight-year old boy. Son of a coach-builder. Wearing a stolen waistcoat. In his three pockets were a walnut, an almond, a coin from the South known as a lockster, a brass button, a toothpick, a quill, a crab-apple, and a length of ribbon which smelt of urine.*

*5. Too shy to state her name. A female probably aged four. In her pockets were three bone buttons and a shell. And a poorly fashioned artificial flower made of painted canvas that tried hard to simulate a rose.*

*6. Qualey Vestris. A bold letter "A" printed on a square of parchment, and the crumbs of the crust of a brown loaf of bread were found in her pockets. It was implied that she wanted to learn to read and that she understood to learn to read you had to understand the alphabet. She had to start to learn the alphabet by knowing its first letter. With the first letter of the alphabet safely in her pocket, and with a crust of bread there also, she felt she was situated to become a useful citizen of the new post-war world. She asked for help in looking for the second letter of the alphabet.*

*7. Magus Thrift. Her pockets contained three short sticks and a lense to make things look smaller. She argued that the lense meant that she could have space to see more. She was not understood.*

*8. A smallish boy with a stutter and a birthmark on his forehead shaped like a cockerel. In his trouser pockets were unripe figs and seven short straws for fixing a wager.*

*9. A girl aged five years old who wept through embarrassment, believing she would be punished for having full pockets in a dress she was wearing that rightly belonged to her sister named Mandolina. She had seven cherry stones, one for each day of the week, a blunt knife blade, a nose-rag and a glob of grease that once upon a time could have been edible.*

*10. A young crippled girl. Ran away before offering identity. Name unintelligible. In her pockets were a nose-rag, a black stone, and a length of looped string fastened with a copper wire kept because of its green verdigris colour. She was very favourably disposed to the colour green.*

*11. A small girl who carried her possessions in her hands since she said her mother made her dresses and never had enough cloth left over to make pockets. She held a piece of dried toast and a ceramic marble and a horse chestnut soaked in vinegar. It was holed and threaded through with a knotted leather thong. This examination took place in the conker season.*

*12. A diamond and a razor in its case. The two items, she said, denoted an assassin. Neither were real. And she did not understand the meaning of the word "assassin". She said she enjoyed the word because it reminded her of snakes. She refused to say her name and was put in a cell for further investigation.*

*13. Poorly Maiden. She had a painted wooden ball used in the gambling game "Sevens and Elevens."*

*14. A sweet made from honey, and a horse chestnut soaked in vinegar, holed and threaded through with a knotted leather thong. This examination took place in the conker season.*

*15. A glass phial, origin unknown, perhaps belonging at one time to a medical man. It was known that her mother had been sick.*

*16. Pills of unspecified nature deemed too risky to ingest, even in the desire to be a thorough investigator. And a dice with one of the six faces - the side "five" made blank.*

*17. An unnamed boy with pierced ears. In his pocket were three reddish stones and a freshwater mussel shell still stinking of the river.*

*18. Unnamed girl. A short length of rope in her skirt pocket. It had been cut down from a gibbet. "It is for rubbing on my brother's arm where it was withered from a palsy brought about by him sleeping with Apory, my mother's sister."*

*19. Boy without a name. A length of string with some red sealing wax attached was found in his pocket. Along with six rat tails, an oak-gall and three acorns.*

*20. A pencil stub. The pencil had been preserved because it had been used to write on a piece of paper that had been sent to his brother in jail. It was the only contact he had with any of his family. A desperate and useless contact that brought tears to the eyes of the examiners.*

*21. A girl, perhaps three years old. A single earring made of a painted brown wood set with orange and red fragments of glass. It had belonged to her mother.*

*22. Her name was Marly, nothing more. Found in a coal tip. In her pockets were an oak apple, a black stone, and a sword buckle, and a horse chestnut soaked in vinegar, holed and threaded through with a knotted leather thong. This examination took place in the conker season.*

*23. A pacifier "for my sister aged two, who is missing her mother who was gored by a pregnant bear."*

*24.There was sand and rat tails in his pockets. "He had just come from the river."*

*25. A cup handle. No cup. "The child did not know what a cup was."*

*26. The lid of a medicine jar that smelt of calamine lotion. And a yellow stone said to be lucky. And two acorns.*

*27. Maisier Missouri. This child aged perhaps five years old. A small roll of paper wrapped in oiled string, and a horse chestnut soaked in vinegar, holed and threaded through with a knotted leather thong. This examination took place in the conker season.*

**Censorship of toys was 'the first of all evils' said Parmitter**

CATEGORY 48. NEW SURVEILLANCE PURSUED.

**Here is a summation of the findings of Poppea Stilts which has been drawn from her consideration of all three hundred of her collected childrens' pockets. She is still engaged in writing up her ultimate conclusions.**

*1. There was a propensity of stones, many of them water-worn flints, most of them kept in a pocket because of their unusual shape or colour.*

*2. There was a propensity of rags, undoubtedly kept for every possible use, but those uses were undoubtedly concentrated on wiping the nose or wrapping around a wound.*

[110] *3. There was a propensity of acorns. Children are always fascinated by acorns. They are like miniature buildings, like rotondas and cupolas, domed structures completed with a spike at the top, perfectly rounded out, complete, and settled architecturally in a cup, snugly based and bottomed out, very satisfying in their completeness.*

*4. There was a propensity of oak-apples, curiously organic spheres, perfected by nature, growing mysteriously on old oak trees.*

*5. There was a propensity of river mud, glaucous, malleable and smelling of decay.*

*6. There was a propensity of galls.*

*7. There were an unusual number of freshwater crayfish heads.*

*8. There were numerous small turnips, many of them bitten into experimentally.*

*9. There were plentiful numbers of almond stones. There were numerous horse-chestnuts bored through to be fitted with a string or twine or leather thong. The examination often took place in the conker season.*

*10. There were more than a few rats' tails tied together in fives. Apparently a fashionable thing to do among small children at this time.*

**Pleased with the success of her collection of the contents of the pockets of children, Poppae Stilts went into partnership with Opsinger Dedestry to expand her research into the contents of satchels, pencil-boxes, lunch-boxes, handbags, purses and wallets. Their combined research was heavy-handed and demanding and there was some resistance due to the inevitable invasion of privacy. It built up considerable personal animosity towards Opsinger Dedestry.**

**Perhaps this incident encouraged other official bodies to interfere, though in some cases, jealousy was a prime cause; there was much animosity that the toys project ostensibly organized by children was so well funded and collated. Official pressure was such that an enforced demonstration to scrutinize the toy collection was insisted upon, and dramatically made manifest by a surprise raid on the collection housed in the Book Depository Building by anthropologists who insisted that the toy collection illegally haboured anthropological items that were public property and necessary for research elsewhere. They confiscated twelve items.**

CATEGORY 49. TROUBLING CONFISCATIONS.

**Twelve Toy items confiscated from the Book Depository Building Collection.**

*1. A doll taken from a child's cot on the excuse it was made of mammoth ivory probably made by a doctor to indicate anatomical weaknesses in royal children suffering from bone marrow diseases on the principle that mammoth ivory was a sympathetic material for royal bones.*

*2. A hollow extendible pea-shooter on the excuse it was really a collapsible gentleman's brass ferruled walking cane from Arbiter Fleece, once a reputable veterinary college professor. It had no place being in the possession of children.*

*3. pair of bent tweezers used by children for catching fleas on the excuse it was a two hundred year-old pair of sugar tongs and fleas were drawn to sugar, especially when manufactured from sugar-beet.*

*4. A spring spiked with a stuffed mouse on the excuse it was once part of a wooden and metal mousetrap.*

[112] *5. A broken pink parasol, taken for reasons unknown, perhaps simply because it was attractive and coveted.*

*6. A ragged bear mask that was supposed to have been owned by a Southern lady of notorious repute.*

*7. A clothes-stand for dolls' clothes used by children in the Fallgoing Orphanage for crippled girls and now considered, after a scraping down, to be a platinum and gilt-coated bottle-rack from the kitchens of the Blue Hotel in KettleMaine.*

*8. Three large wooden mushroom-shaped objects branded with numbers used by small girls as doll-stools but now believed to be hat molds.*

*9. A scratched portrait of a moustached man wearing earrings used by children in games of The Hungry Giant, now believed to be a portrait of Umber Kane, the fiddle player.*

*10. The head of a cassowary made of coloured plaster and dressed in a paper skirt used as a puppet, now considered an heirloom of the Astringent Family who built the Estable Bridge over the Slow Madder River.*

*11. A purple flag used as a curtain to a make-believe sentry box for soldiers. Purple was a sign of privilege for lawyers.*

*12. A bowl of kerridge.*

**The collection of toys belonging to the ginger-haired Eerio Padebourne, the blonde-haired boy, Irium Bostero, the black-haired boy Jendro Hisloper, and the brown-haired, Stoolie Goltdown, was growing too large for the scullery of Izek Bable in the orphanage at Thessel, in the foothills of the Wouverain Mountains. It was becoming necessary to find a new storage space.**

**The closeness of the four children to the pastry-cook Izek Bable, not surprising considering that they all lived in the same orphanage buildings, irritated Opsinger Dedestry. He**

was becoming jealous of the relationship, thinking it would jeopardize his attempts for self-advertisement in his journey to become a professional Historian. Knowing that the woman of his acquaintance, Loadstar Fives, was related by marriage to Lutumariner, the acting leader of the Historians Project, he offered her a large inducement out of the Toys Funding Finances to become his secretary with special responsibilities to arrange the future public exhibition of Toys. Loadstar Fives joined the affiliation. Within a week she had fully acquainted herself with the dubious ambitions of Opsinger Dedestry, whose major agenda seemed to be self-advancement. Seeking to find favour with him, having witnessed the element of water as a subject area, she had suggested the element of air and thus the condition of anti-gravity toys.

# AIR

CATEGORY 50. ESCAPE ONE.

Gravity toys, often of a foreign origin, supposedly from the South, as it was always considered that innovations started in the South, became familiar. Even the origins of the Continental Wars was considered, probably erroneously, to be a Southern invention. An envy of the South's apparent ability to innovate was inflammatory. These wooden toys were all motored by gravity that had been temporarily resisted in some way in order to create arrested movement that could be released at will when desired. It is not improbable that these toys, suddenly flourishing, owed their existence in attempts to copy foreign models, nominally Southern, in order to better them. Jealousy was obviously an incitement.
Confumo, initially with his tongue in his cheek no doubt, even suggested that gravity was a Southern invention. He exaggerated the claim, even humorously suggesting that

[114] **Gravity made seas. The mechanism for such a claim was exceedingly difficult to fathom.**

**Confumo threw further wood on the fire by suggesting other outrageous things. As an enthusiastic family man, he suggested that the human orgasm in matters of sexual activity was essential for both parents, because it excited a substance into the blood stream that helped substantially bond parentage to make certain that mutually encouraged good child-rearing that protected a child's future welfare at least for seven years for the child's benefit. It was considered that for seven years at least a child seriously needed its parents' care to become self-supporting. As regards the child, two parents were always better than one. The excitement of mutually experiencing orgasm kept parents together to appreciate one another. Hence of course the idea of the seven-year itch. After seven years, apparently mutual orgasm diminished in couples long used to one another's company. It diminished in strength and frequency, as did parental bonding in general. But by that time, it was possible that the child was better prepared to survive alone.**

*1. A popular gravity toy was a man, nominally wearing a blue hat, climbing down a ladder using the insteps of his feet. You reversed the toy for the man in the blue hat to climb up the ladder. Thus gravity in reverse.*

*2. A woman standing on a strip of green grass in a red skirt beating a carpet. Each beat of her stick ratcheted the next beat.*

*3. Six pheasants pecking at a sheaf of wheat on a farmyard pavement. A weighted wooden ball beneath the representable farmyard pavement, when agitated, made each pheasant severally dip its head to peck.*

*4. Eight white doves pecking at grain. This toy operated with the same mechanism as item three.*

*5. A fat woman lifting a purple skirt, crouching to urinate. This vulgarity was popular with small boys.*

*6. Two children with pig-tails rocking a see-saw.*

*7. A green woodpecker on a spring sliding down a pole.*

*8. Two chickens walking down a wooden slope.*

*9. A pink and white stork stooping to drink. As the wooden bird stooped, small children invariably made a slurping noise with the tongue against the roof of the mouth.*

*10. A fat man riding a unicycle.*

*11. A fat woman beating her husband with a rolling pin.*

*12. A fat man drinking from a bottle.*
*In some versions, the bottle was labeled "alcoholic".*

CATEGORY 51. ESCAPE TWO.

**Flying paper darts. A large category from which a small selection has been made.**

*1. A paper dart made from school graph paper that had been scribbled on with a few figures and then abandoned. The figures suggest someone had been calculating the sum of three fifteens.*

*2. A dart folded from a stiff blue paper that bore marks of greasy food. A few bread-crumbs were attached, perhaps from a buttered currant bun.*

*3. A paper dart folded from a love letter. The love letter had been written in a mature hand by a woman obsessed with her own pain, to a woman who appeared to possess a lower educational level than her correspondent. As was perfectly in keeping with its secondary usage, the folded paper dart totally ignored any comprehension of the frustration and sorrow contained in the letter. Turning the letter into a flying object did not release any of the pain. The dart when thrown against the wind flew very well. "It is a pity that its success as a flying dart could not have been mirrored in the sentiments of the love letter."*

*4. A school paper impregnated with the watermark of a bee carrying excess pollen in its pollen bags. The watermark had been devised to indicate the prosperity of the school, the need to emulate apian industry, the well-known cooperation of a hive, and the capacity to harvest nourishing knowledge.*

*5. A paper dart made from a section of parchment scribbled hastily with the markings of a bird that, considering the length of its wing-span, could have been an albatross. But this is unlikely since the albatross is a rare bird inland. Some say that it is a fictitious bird only ever seen over a sea, and since a sea does not exist, the whole issue is a fiction.*

*6. A paper dart folded from a page of a book of anatomy featuring the heart in detail. The heart was drawn with three large ventricles and presumably, if drawn from nature, must have vastly incapacitated its owner. The paper was heavy and did not fly so well as a folded dart.*

*7. A blank white sheet clumsily folded and refolded as though its maker did not know how to make a flying missile.*

*8. A sheet of yellow paper marked with eyes.*

*9. A half sheet of a map showing the foothills of the Goranga Mountains north of the Wouverain Range.*

*10. A paper dart made from a sheet of red wrapping paper that had apparently been flecked with bleach. Could the dart have been made in a laundry?*

*11. A sheet of white paper covered in a school writing exercise, where the pressure of the pen in the hands of the writer, combined with the excessive amounts of ink being used, had dampened and thus softened the paper, and had frequently caused the pen to pierce the paper.*

*12. A sheet of grey paper where the missile manufacturer had sketched the missile's imaginary flying pilot and his female companion who had a scarf blowing back at right angles from her naked body. The missile manufacturer obviously had a certain desire that might have associated sexual activity with vigorous flight.*

*13. A paper dart made from a title page torn from a book of mathematics.*

*14. A paper dart made from a page torn from a pencil-written diary, where on a certain March 15th, a lurid encounter with a flying lizard was described as though it was a direct personal experience. The flying lizard was pierced with twenty-three wounds and died at the feet of a statue of a military man who was identified with a prominent quiff that suggested he was an ancient hero who was murdered in a boat on a beach, a great many years ago.*

*15. A paper dart made from a thick sheet of brown paper, known as "grocer's paper", that at one time could have wrapped some greasy substance like butter.*

*16. A paper dart made from a white sheet of paper that was spattered with red spots that could have been blood.*

*17. A paper dart made from a small sheet of blue paper marked with the names of six locally famous orators, Thoro' Spellery, Marbus, Okky Smarts, Buderow, Cardobus, and Epsie Cardoma Borgo. It is possible that the connection between these six worthies was gravity. They had variously been advocates for and against cases of defenestration, judicial hanging, a juggler's pension, a mountain-climbing accident, a victim of a collapsed tower and a theatrical entertainer impersonating a bird.*

*18. A sheet of white paper where the fold lines used to make the flying dart, had been penciled in.*

*19. Two pieces of paper stitched together with blue thread, the stitch lines folded into the dart in such a way as to give the missile a centre gravity line, the blue thread being heavier than the brown paper.*

*20. A blank page spattered in fly-droppings, torn from a book, and scribbled over with the words "Clandestine Report."*

*21. A sheet of very expensive-looking paper impregnated with a scent that still lingered after some thirty years.*

**Sophia Meeds is anxious that restoration work is to be made as regards the fifteen items she is prepared to lend to the Wouverain Toys Project. She wishes to employ at her own expense, a restorer. This restorer needs to offer evidence of the restoration work. The items have lost much colour and Eerio is adamant that the colour cannot be faithfully restored**

## CATEGORY 52. ENVELOPE CORRESPONDENCE.

**Envelope collections. Unopened envelopes were treasured. Opening them was considered a privilege.**

*1. An envelope filled with red dots, the sort that once upon a more prosperous time, indicated the sale of an object.*

*2. An envelope of blue triangles that might have related to the retailing of soft cheeses.*

*3. A brown envelope normally used for sending confidential letters filled with black spots.*

*4. A four times folded-over envelope filled with dust from under a green carpet. The dust particles were certainly green.*

*5. Grass seed not found in temperate climates wrapped up in a screw of graph paper and encased in a yellow envelope.*

*6. An envelope of stolen pepper that had lain so long, the pepper no longer made you sneeze.*

*7. An envelope of dust from powdered oak-apples believed to have been pulverized in preparation to make ink. The writing in a childish hand on the outside of the envelope read, "Ink for Contracts".*

*8. An envelope that, according to what was written in pencil on its inside flap, had once contained smoke.*

## CATEGORY 53. MORE CONSPIRATORIAL CORRESPONDENCE.

### Paper constructions believed to have been made to create sounds.

*1. Two pieces of stiff white paper attached to a piece of cardboard such that a quick downward flick by a child's hand would create a loud sound. The sound of a slap.*

*2. A funnel of thick brown paper shaped like a trumpet. The mouthpiece was much chewed and smelt of aniseed.*

*3. Two roughly-cut cardboard circles threaded on a loop of string, which, it was believed, could make a whirring sound if swung with sufficient vigour.*

[120] CATEGORY 54. THE FUNNEL AS METAPHOR.

**Various funnels that held a fascination for children on account of their ability to direct small objects into a vessel of some description without spilling. Chaos confined.**

*1. A funnel made of gum-stiffened paper that had once funneled salt.*

*2. A funnel to be worn on the head like a hat. It was big enough to cover the ears of most five-year old children. There was evidence that it was once attached to leather straps to be fastened under the chin.*

*3. A wooden funnel much worn.*

*4. A metal funnel somewhat rusted. To be used in a children's playground.*

*5. A funnel for speaking down when you became angry.*

*6. A small metal funnel found in association with a wooden doll. There was some circumspect evidence that the funnel was used for forced feeding the doll cold pea-soup.*

*7. A funnel for small females to pee through to pretend they were boys.*

**A rival toy collection has been started in Esterwary by a Collective who felt certain that their collection of toys was superior to that devised by Eedio Padebourne, and suggested that there was no room for two such collections to be put together within a hundred miles of PastonCumber. They wrote that "We should come to an agreement to share and combine our efforts. We have received offers of a buy-out from a certain Opsinger Dedestry who claims he is the overriding authority in this matter".**

Eddio Padebourne wrote back, saying, "We have no wish in any respect to share our collection and the eventual intended associated exhibition, and we find your intransigence unbelievable and that you are trespassing on our territory." They replied. "Surely the post-war public wants to see a truly representative toys exhibition and your selfishness of not wishing to share, will demean the interest. You will be hearing from our lawyers. We could come to some arrangement to make a formal financial settlement."

And there the correspondence stopped.

CATEGORY 55. POCKET-KNIVES.

A haphazard collection of variously broken pocket-knives discovered in a school-house. A pocket-knife at the very utmost was a challenging phenomenon. It was a dangerous item for a child to observe and certainly to possess and hold. These pocket knives were scribbled on with coloured pencils, desensitising them somewhat, making them to be no longer conscientiously considered to be instrumentally associated with danger and death. They were in this present context not so associated as to be considered as working tools. In some instances their original fanciful fastidiousness, inlaid often with mica and coloured glass, intimated that they should not be taken too seriously in the first place.

*1. With six blades of different sizes, four blunt, three rusty and one twisted.*

*2. With five blades of different sizes, two blunt, two with grossly serrated edges and a small rusted corkscrew.*

*3. With two blades of different sizes, both blunt, a small corkscrew snapped off at the base, and a damaged screwdriver.*

*4. With two blades of different sizes, one snapped off at the base, a small corkscrew and a rusted screwdriver and a damaged spoon used to stir fennel in a glass of beer.*

*5. With two blades of different sizes, both broken at the base where they met the handle, a small corkscrew and a screwdriver and a twisted spoon used to stir fennel in a glass of beer and a small rusted fork used to stab meat to bring it to your mouth.*

*6. With a broken knife, a twisted fork and a loose rattling spoon and a gimlet.*

*7. With a rusted bottle opener and a rusted corkscrew.*

*8. With a thin rusty stiletto blade and a dog-whistle whose efficacy was in doubt because if it sounded at all, its high pitch was inaudible to a human ear and apparently inaudible also to a dog's ear as well it seemed.*

## ALTITUDE

**Izek Bable, the orphanage pastry cook, took the ginger-haired Eerio Padebourne rock-climbing. Eerio Padebourne became intrigued by the mountains. Forever fascinated by the possibility of new categories, he tried to discover how to categorize toys by altitude. The Wouverain Mountains were essentially bare of substantial vegetation and the toys found were largely prized for their supposed anthropomorphic characteristics, treasured by children to reveal the spirit, it was said, imprisoned in roots, gnarled branches and rocks and stones.**

CATEGORY 56. DESIRE TO CLIMB HIGHER.

**Here is a record of the toys discovered by Izek Bable and Eerio Padebourne three and a half thousand feet up The Aptitude Mountain.**

*1. A stone whose shape had suggested a head with a long nose. Children had drawn an eye and a tongue on its left-hand side.*

*2. A flying figure made from a tree root wrapped around with bracken.*

*3. A figure with a long tongue.*

*4. The end of a branch suggesting a wolf leaping.*

*5. A rock cloud in the shape of a fox.*

*6. A root strongly suggesting women with braided hair.*

*7. A hermaphrodite figure with three breasts.*

*8. The root of a pine tree representing to Eerio a woman sitting by a window waiting for her lover, a fanciful image no doubt brought to mind by Seridan's painting of The Morose West Wind in the PastonCumber Gallery of Heroines.*

*9. A wild pig with two tails.*

*10. A cow with a broken horn.*

### CATEGORY 57. DESIRE TO CLIMB EVEN HIGHER STILL

**Here is a record of the toys found above four and a half thousand feet on a second mountain, Mount Asperol.**

*1. A black dung beetle with the legs removed to be worn as a brooch.*

*2. A goat horn smoothed by the animal rubbing its skull on a rock ledge.*

*3. A root shaped like a sheep with large udders.*

*4. A root bole shaped like a blind lamb.*

*5. A tree branch representing a goat condemned to death by gravity and blindness.*

*6. A stone shaped like a cave monster.*

*7. A cave child made of ice kept in a rock shelter to avoid melting.*

*8 A root in the shape of a kestrel with large eyes.*

*9. An eagle with a snake in its claws made of pine roots.*

*10. A collection of pine cones strung with string.*

**It was noted that in the many cemeteries of the Wouverain Mountains, there were several graves of orphan children. The women of the Wouverain Mountain Community had spent much harassed time and effort trying to discover the identity of orphans of the recent wars. In part there had been some success. Many orphans had been taken in and cosseted. Orphan corpses had been exhumed from temporary graves and reburied in Wouverain Mountain graveyards. On many occasions, toys had been buried with these children. With circumspect sensitive attention many of these toys had been reverently untangled from the arms of a dead child, and had received special care and included in the Toy Project collection.**

CATEGORY 58: TO CLIMB AS HIGHER AS POSSIBLE

**Here is a record of the toys found above five thousand feet on a third mountain in the Hollery Range of the Wouverain Heights, where arsenic had been mined for five hundred years. Arsenic here came out of the ground as a yellow powder.**

*1. Arsenic powder frozen in icicles. To be preserved in a cold cave.*

*2. A pretend ice boat.*

*3. A snow child made of a ceramic coloured yellow with arsenic crystals.*

*4. A clutch of bear claws.*

*5. The teeth of a snow leopard.*

*6. A wolf skin stained red.*

*7. An ice-cairn.*

*8. Two ice cairns.*

*9.A rock shaped like an anvil.*

*10.A stretch of ice rails.*

*11. A meteorite.*

**Izek Bable, the orphanage pastry-cook, was accused of illegal abuse of the ginger-haired boy Eerio Padebourne. Rumour suggested he was teaching the boy to cook pastries in the seclusion of a mountain hut on the Hollery Range Mountains. There was talk of mushroom collecting. Was this code for other calumnies? Izek Bable vehemently denied the charge. And where did any legal register ever suggest that the teaching of cooking pastries in association with mushrooms be regarded as illegal abuse? Lutumariner, the acting head of the Historians Project, wishing no trace of impropriety should sully the project, played for safety against the now publically patronized Toy Project, and he demanded that Izek Bable should be stood down from the Toy Project and be denied all further contact with children, especially orphan children.**

[126] It was becoming very apparent that the Toys Project of the three boys was becoming increasingly public with the expansion of the public funding, the involvement of the historian Lutumariner and now gossip about impropriety. But not all the publicity was negative. Many sections of the public curiosity were aroused, and a wish to be involved was evident. The ubiquity of the importance of toys for children, both orphans and non-orphans, was strong. It touched a chord in most people's sensitivity. One inquiry came from a reputed designer of exhibitions, Tholas Meakas, and he offered his assistance. He contacted Izek Bable who convened a meeting before disappearing into some form of removal of himself from the orphanage so as not to create further embarrassment for everyone who felt that they might be associated.

## CATEGORY 59. TOYS AS EVIDENCE OF DEPRAVITY.

Opsinger Dedestry, in his ambitious bid for recognition as a Historian, could benefit from Izek Bable's apparent disgrace. The reputation of a supposed rival had been damaged. It has always been a certain way to discredit an enemy or an opponent by bringing up an accusation of the abuse of children. Now Opsinger Dedestry exacerbated opinion by publishing a list of toys that he itemized as "toys as evidence of depravity". The list was a calumny in the context. Eerio, determined to discredit Opsinger Dedestry's accusation, publically exhibited toy items he could discover associated with the items of so-called depravity, suitably credited with relevant notices saying explicitly that they were exhibited to refute abhorrent accusations. It was not a wise thing to do, since, despite other ambiguities, it was bound to be seen as a provocation.

1. *A leather coil.*

2. *A short stick.*

*3. A bag of grease.*

*4. A softened length of candle.*

*5. A pair of torn trousers with a pocket stuffed with thistle.*

*6. A pair of red trousers with the shoulder-straps removed.*

*7. A pair of blue trousers with the buttons removed.*

*8. A plait of human hair smeared in raspberry preserve.*

*9. A metal cone six inches high.*

*10. A striped jacket.*

**The items on the list self-evidently did indeed offer themselves to ambiguity which defused Dedestry's intention. All in all it has been agreed that Opsinger Dedestry's plan had backfired, though there were certain conservative authorities that persisted in making adverse publicity. It has been strongly inferred that Opsinger Dedestry himself may have been directly responsible for the initial rumour of depravity. He began to argue in public that cooking pastries was a crude form of code used by the females of the Wouverain Mountains. It was a shameless form of defence. He certainly made himself enemies in the matriarchies of the Wouverain Mountains.**

**In a further defence against calumny supported by Lutumariner, the boys were now placed in the charge of the secretary Loadstar Fives who was promoted to chief archivist of the Toys Project. Lutumariner was said to be an uncle by marriage of Loadstar Fives. She rented rooms in a Book Depository Building stocked a century before by military navigators and cartographers, a great many of them friends and work partners of the Historian Confumo. There was still evidence of the building's previous occupation in maps and plans of unknown territories still pinned to the green walls. The unknown territories appeared**

 now as white blank areas on some of the maps, reminding viewers of the objections of many parties across the border in the South whose memories were still full of hostility. Some of these maps also demonstrated an interest in the existence of an apocryphal sea in tracing out routes through the arid deserts of the Far South. There was also evidence of railway tracks with complex systems of signals and multiple points for changing directions.

Loadstar Fives employed carpenters to build shelving and she began to sort out the collection of toys that had accumulated, starting in Room One with Categories One to Seventeen and continuing in Room Two with Categories Nineteen to Twenty-Two that dealt with Music.

Loadstar Fives began to consider necessary limits to the collection. It was becoming expensive to exhibit everything. The potential was endless. "Everything in the world could be considered a toy", she said. But nonetheless she paid serious attention to the boy Eerie Padebourne's taxonomies.

The funding benefactors began to insist on a date for the future exhibition of the toys. They allocated an increase of funding if the catalogue could be printed in colour. Opsinger Dedestry made attempts to court and seduce Loadstar Fives, knowing she was related to Lutumariner. It was known that Loadstar Fives was anxious to have a baby. She was now forty-three. And it was apparent that Lutumariner had suddenly taken a very serious private interest in the Toys Project. Observers took every opportunity to connect these events namely, taxonomies, structured shelving, the apocryphal sea, catalogues, babies, and Lutumariner's sudden intense interest, especially in the Jill-in-a-Box toy. Significantly increased attention in dolls, previously only a minor concern but now noted with some considerable fascination, was undoubtedly growing.

And again the Jill-in-a-Box toy that, when opened, provided such a stimulating female laugh, had again gone missing. It was rumoured that Lutumariner had permanently purloined the toy in question. Dedestry's fascination with the Jill-in-a Box toy was becoming obsessive. He connected it to Esquila Fontenay.

## GRAVE TOYS

Eerie Padebourne's journeys into the Wouverain Mountains were starting to create yet more new categories.

CATEGORY 60. ELEMENTS OF SADNESS.

Toys discovered on the graves of children in the Wouverain Mountains who had died on account of fatal goitres, created by an iodine deficiency. Many of these children were discovered to be war-orphans.

*1. A thin-necked bottle containing coloured beads.*

*2. A miniature wineglass full of honey eaten by ants and flies.*

*3. A glass walking stick full of sweets which exposure and moistness in the grave had reduced to a mush of coloured sugar.*

*4. A toy discovered on the grave of a child who had died on account of fatal gallstones.*

*5. A necklace of small wooden balls.*

The rival collection had appointed Periculum Arretes to research toys from the East. We understand from the designer Stipony Aforesaid that the Periculum Arrestes has a workshop in Skittering which is preparing to manufacture fakes made after the cessation of hostilities. This was considered unacceptable.

[130] **Periculum Arrestes said, "You do not have any authorization to decide what is true and what is a fake and in the manufacture of toys – at best a most ephemeral activity - there are no rules or deciding factors to be considered."**

**Peone Stiffkey declared. "It is unfitting that in association with the interests of minors, Lutumariner's moral turpitude is anathema." What possible moral turpitude could be at stake here?**

CATEGORY 61. GRAVE TOYS.

**Toys discovered on the graves of children in the Wouverain Mountains who had died on account of fatal arsenic poisoning.**

*1. A yellow doll with feathered wings.*

*2. A yellow doll with an open mouth painted red in the inside.*

*3. A winged figure with yellow feet.*

CATEGORY 62. LIGHTNING STRIKE.

*1. A jar full of blue coloured water containing wooden fish.*

*2. An artificial candle.*

*3. A peeled white stick, broken in five places to make six jags.*

*4. A smoking coal in a bird-shaped iron basket.*

CATEGORY 63. AVALANCHES.

*1. Balloons for flying away. Babylouse said she was prepared. At the suggestion of a movement of the earth preparatory to an avalanche beneath her feet, she strapped six black balloons around her waist in a sort of corset of wires and whalebone, and lifted herself by way of pulleys off the floor, clinging to the rails on her walls and thus hoisting herself off the ground to be free of rumbling rocks and trembling stones. However at the time of the Avida Frosts, she was not quick enough and she perished, the toy balloons not being able to support her weight.*

*2. A pile of white painted stones. There were five of them, the Doctor, the Spicer, th Eggplant, the Saucer and the Mint. They were arranged in a line from her front door to the ditch at her backgate. Painted very white by weekly licks of new distemper, they were clearly visible and when the avalanche threatened, easy to follow in the dark out to the ditch and thus to safety. She was an intrepid and valorous child, the doughty heroine of her street. They took to calling her The Insouciant. The five stones were laid on her grave.*

*3. A bunch of dried laurel leaves tied with faded red ribbons. Laurel was the plant that, tied into a wreath. was worn by poets and literary heroes and no literary figure has ever been overtaken by an avalanche. Tobacco Caterham's laurel wreath was considered a toy.*

*4. A collection of love letters from the bereaved mother of a dead child to the dead child's dead father. They had been covered in mould and mouse droppings.*

## CATEGORY 64. TOYS DISCOVERED ON THE GRAVES OF CHILDREN IN THE WOUVERAIN MOUNTAINS WHO HAD DIED FROM HYPOTHERMIA AND EXPOSURE.

*1. Blankets embroidered with dogs and cats. Sideroi said that they barked and mewed every evening when they were not fed.*

*2. A hat that could be turned inside out to suit the weather.*

*3. A doll wearing many clothes.*

*4. Gloves embroidered with butterflies.*

*5. Mittens.*

*6. Mittens for the feet with five red tassels for extra symbolic warmth.*

**Whilst in the Wouverain Mountains searching through the graves of those children who had suffered altitude illnesses and died, Eerio Padebourne again, after seven years, was reunited with Esquila Fontenay. She was the girl who had been seen on the damp grass near the fence at the back of the Orphanage orchard and had her Jill-in-the-Box stolen. That was the Jill-in-a-Box who laughed like a Queen. There was an immediate look of recognition between Esquila and Eerio though some four years had elapsed since they had previously encountered one another.**

**Esquila was plain looking in general terms but had ferocious eyes. She had a plump nose and plump lips. She took Eerio cemetery-travelling. Eerio and Esquila ate together and quarreled together and, just like her still missing Jill-in-a-Box, she laughed like a Queen. It was apparent to Eerio that one day Esquila would be the Superintendant of the Wouverain Mountains. And he himself might necessarily turn out to be a repeat Lutumariner and that might also suggest he might also follow Lutumariner's profession and become an authoritative Historian. And, without a doubt, Esquila's enthusiasm to find the Sea was influential in Eerio's imagination. Maybe, he dreamt, that the final definitive end of the wars would be heralded by the discovery of the missing and mythic Sea. Maybe the finding of the Sea would be the major characteristic of the Post-War Civilization.**

**From that time Eerio began to hand over the major responsibilities of the Toy Project to Jendro Hisloper and he**

started to prepare himself for his determination to lead an expedition to the South to find if indeed that there might be a Sea. It was Esquila Fontenay who showed Eerio the grave of her mother and from whom Eerio learnt he might be her mother's son and of course that she was his sister. In all this he was to be recognised as Lutumariner's grandchild. It was said that Esquila Fontenay's mother had lost her legs, travelling too fast in a Racing Cart on the rail-tracks of the Wouverain Mountains.

The ginger-haired boy, Eerio Padebourne with the blonde-haired boy, Irium Bostero, were spending considerable amounts of time with communities of mountain-people, porters, carriers and guides, many of whom were exiles from the recent Continental Troubles whose families had fled to the mountains to escape pursuers. Entirely disillusioned by the activities of warring men, a considerable number of these communities had for a great many years been made up almost entirely of females, making largely well-organized matriarchies who had little use for men apart from fertilization. They captured a likely candidate and used him as a stud till they either tired of him, or his apparent siring of infants exceeded a given number. Thirty years back that number was ten, now it was a hundred. They volunteered the used-up and rejected male to a single partner if any female was willing to take him on, or else he was summarily expelled from the Wouverain Mountains.

Male children were often exposed to the cold in the mountains and swiftly perished, or if a mother insisted on keeping a male child, mother and child were given subsistence money for six months and expelled from the community. Many agreed to serve in colonies in the valleys. Because of their considerable beauty and strong character many of these women were soon married. But marriage was soon considered demeaning and certainly unnecessary. It was said that some of the exposed children were delivered to the valley orphanages. It was rumoured that the three orphaned children Eerio Padebourne

[134] and Irium Bostero and Jendro Hisloper had been subjects in this strategy.

Learning of the expedition of the two boys Eerio Padebourne and Irium Bostero into the female communities of the mountains, Lutumariner asked for monthly reports of the investigation and created opportunities for the collection of toys to be moved en masse to the Book Depository Building where he made frequent visits to inspect the collected toys. It was apparent that he was looking for something. It was noted that representative images of the female figure were desirable and avidly collected.

Eerio Padebourne and Irium Bostero slowly developed relationships with several of these matriarchial communities, fully explaining their wish to build one day a foundation for post-Continental Troubles History complete with scholarships and exhibitions. The youthful nature of Eerio Padebourne and Irium Bostero and Jendro Hisloper appeared to not intimidate the females of the Wouverain Mountains.

Lutumariner had apparently come to the conclusion that the ultimate toy was the doll. The doll was the representation of the self. What more could be more important or more relevant? Or indeed more interesting? Automaton, robot, mannikin, scarecrow. Many Gods were made manifest in a human representational form, give or take one or two other animal adjuncts or characteristics such as a lion's mane, an elephant's trunk, an owl's wisdom, a snake's tongue. These adjuncts were considered unimportant and local.

Entirely independently, Eerio Padebourne came to the same conclusion as Lutumariner that the ultimate toy was the doll. This situation was largely confirmed after Eerio Padebourne had met Esquila Fontenay. She had convinced him. Though still collecting toys of every description, Eerio began to concentrate on dolls. He instructed his companions to do the same. Irium Botero who had started his fascination with toys by collecting sticks, started collecting dolls, and his dolls tended to be stick-like and masculine. For Jendro Hisloper

**most of his discoveries had been ball-like and feminine. All three, Eerio Padebourne, Irium Botero and Jendro Hisloper now trooped the country far and wide, though normally always within sight of the Wouverain Mountains, however distant and misty, and almost invisible. All three children now steadily collected dolls.**

**Here are descriptions of some rudimentary dolls which indicated how people were starting to think of a newly focused interest in Toys.**

CATEGORY 65. SOME RUDIMENTARY DOLLS.

*1. Three sticks tied closely together with a greasy twine, the outer two sticks were smaller than the third. A battered wooden skittle ball from a school bowling alley had been lopsidedly glued to one end of the smallest stick, on which a fortuitous horizontal gash had incurred in a long ago skittle-alley match. It had provided the rudimentary doll with a mouth.*

*2. A bunch of seven unsharpened pencils painted yellow, three of them still with erasers at one end. The pencils had clumsily been glued together and dipped in sheep reddle.*

*3. A short pole with a head and diminutive genitals made of paper-paste from the pages of old school exercise books chewed with a mouthful of gooseberry juice. The gooseberry pips were still visible in the corrugations of the disproportionately large scrotal sac. There was something here that might possibly indicate an origin of gooseberry bush-birth mythologies as in the boast of a small child who might say, "My grandmother told me that I was born under a gooseberry bush".*

*4. Hands made of chewed wood, fingers separated out from the chewed fibres and bound delicately with black thread and dipped in beeswax.*

*5. Bird bones to make a ribcage – the whole very delicate and kept in a lidless box on a shelf beside a bed.*

**Lutumariner, many many years before, when he was about twenty-three years of age, at a Truce-Meeting between warring combatants, had met Perpetua, the mythical matriarch of the Wouverain Mountains. He was just a little older than she was. Lutumariner at that time was a subsidiary assistant to a minor diplomat. He was allowed to only use green ink on inferior paper destined for the latrines or to hold fatty substances, for his correspondence. He was not considered as being important. Perpetua was herself low down in the hierarchy of assistants to the Wouverain Matriarchy. Lutumariner was certainly then a Historian but his great project of The Great History was still some forty-five years away, so far in the future distance it was almost as invisible as those blue distant Wouverain Mountains were from PastonCumber.**

**Lutumariner and Perpetua lived together for three years. She wanted him to make a history of the Wouverain Sisterhood in its infancy. And, she joked, he could certainly hold a pen and knew the meanings of such words as "chronology", and "millennium", and "deja vue". They fell in love. Agenda Fontenay was born and soon after that event, her mother Perpetua became acclaimed as an athlete and soon after that she lost her legs at Wouverain Reach. Losing her legs at a Chariot Festival was considered a sort of martyrdom and she was elevated into the Upper Regions of the Wouverain Sisterhood. Henceforth she was a honoured cripple.**
**Then the truces were broken and the Times collapsed again and war claimed precedence over babies and love and sacrificed legs and Lutumariner and Perpetua parted company. Lutumariner lived in honorable employment in PastonCumber. Perpetua was kidnapped by sympathizers, and being wounded, kept secluded, safely guarded. The daughter Agenda was raised in total female company. And thus Lutumariner and Perpetua rarely if ever communicated again unless it was on official paper with green ink.**

**The fascination with self-image, man or woman, male or female, from now on dominated the Toy Project. Walking, sleeping, running, flying, comatose, conscious, unconscious, expressing queenly laughter on a throne or miserably exploited in a dull ditch, the number of dolls increased. Lutumariner wanted to revisit memories, even had ideas of rekindling associations. He repeatedly now visited the hostelry on the Richstag Ridge within sight of the Wouverain Mountains, and sat eating oatmeal fritters in a corner of a cabin called "the smaller cage" in memory of Perpetua.**

**Eerio wanted daughters. Lutumariner had fame and reputation. Eerio too wanted fame and reputation. First of all he wanted the Toy Project to be his early calling card in the world, then he wanted to find the sea, then he wanted to become a Historian. His ambitions multiplied.**

CATEGORY 66. RUDIMENTARY DOLL-ITEMS RESCUED FROM DESTRUCTION BY FIRE.

*1. The handle of a sink mop with the remains of the brush as a tuft of ragged wool for hair, and a loop of wire cut and opened up for very small feet. The whole had been dipped up to the metal ferrule that held the ragged hair, in sheep dip to stain it red.*

*2. A broken broom-handle scored around with a blunt instrument to indicate neck, arms, belly, groin, knees and ankles. It had been bored through at one end, and a looped string passed through, so that it might be hung up, maybe to swing on a belt around a waist.*

*3. The broken leg of a school stool, that had been turned on a lathe in a big city and still had the number 34 burnt into its lower left side, with a school ruler nailed at right angles across it for arms. The ruler had been much abused in a school-room, chewed at one end, drilled with small holes around the seven inch-mark, burnt in several places and spatterered in black ink and paint. The nailing was not symmetrical, thus the left arm was four inches long and the right arm eight inches long.*

*4. Two wooden cake spoons tied together face to face, with the inner space filled with an animal fat that had been seasoned with rosemary for remembering.*

*5. Two unmatched wooden cullenders tied together face to face and filled with small white pebbles that had been stuck together with a goat-hoof glue. The whole making some visual semblence of a brain.*

*6. Two battered metal saucepans tied together and still bearing marks of encrusted burnt meat sauce. The saucepans were stuffed with straw and in amongst the straw Deucer found eggshells.*

*7. Two dessert spoons tied together bowl to bowl, in whose shiny polished back surfaces you could see the distorted reflection of your face. The spoons were dye-stamped with the words "The Ratnor". Deucer presumed "The Ratnor" was an eating-house or a hotel. The spoons were delicately joined with red and white plaited twine and kept at a high shine by ardent polishers.*
*Edestry said they were love-spoons, traditionally made in the West as a token of affection by a lover for his beloved, but he was scarcely believed. Formeter later extolled this metaphor with references to mirrors, reflections, the creation of a cupped space, an enclosed heart, high shine, the love knot, inseparable marriage vows, and the sweetness of a wild stawberry dessert. The object was a prize-item for the toy directory and was referred to in the collection as indeed 'The Ratnor". Cosmetrik wrote a fiction where "The Ratnor" was a brothel where all the customers were under twenty-five and all the whores were over fifty. It was considered to be a teaching establishment.*

## CATEGORY 67. ANTHROPOMORPHIC DOLLS.

*1. A root bole that in its own growth suggested human arms and legs that were then cut and bound with twine to approach the form of the human figure, complete, surprisingly, with one ear, two nipples, a navel, a penis and three toes on one foot. It had been associated at a later stage with ceramic additions, and been given an unglazed clay face tied on with wire. The face had large lips and a hexagonal mouth, certainly fashioned by poking a pencil with a hexagonal cross-section through the soft clay.*

## CATEGORY 68. HUMAN SURVIVAL.

**Salient characteristics in the manufacture of dolls. The dolls often had accessories that were assiduously collected.**

*1. Hairpins. A collection of hairpins associated with female dolls with copious hair.*

*2. Keys. A separate collection of keys numbering some two hundred associated with wind-up automaton dolls most of which no longer were operative.*

*3. Meat skewers. Twelve metal meat skewers used to strengthen the backbones of cloth and sawdust dolls.*

*4. Nails and screws, sometimes with metal washers, that, through repeated use, had kept part of the nail or screw free of rust.*

*5. Wedding-rings. Often with a goldsmith's stamp in evidence. Two of these were discovered in the sawdust of a doll's head. Another one was wrapped in tin-foil, and preserved in the approximate region of a doll's heart, which, it is said, is a lttle lower in the body than it is in a human heart.*

## [140] CATEGORY 69. ASSOCIATED ITEMS.

*1. Teeth. Lost teeth made of ceramic; five full sets and three hundred separate individual teeth.*

*2. Bottle caps. Bottle caps with serrated edges and cork interiors – identical bottle caps on which the letters H and G were often visible in green and white enamel. Children had utilised them as badges and medals whilst dressing dolls as war heroes.*

*3. Bottle-stops. Combinations of zinc wire twisted into an double S shape with a white ceramic stopper.*

*4. Metal letters. Shaped possibly as letters of an ancient alphabet, conspicuous amongst them was a rounded M-shape with the down strokes hammered into a wood base. M is the thirteenth letter of the alphabet of twenty-six letters. The middle letter in the alphabet.*

*5. On the front of the body and around the liver on the back of the figure at the base of the backbone. A swatch of black sheep's hair was attached to the head, the armpits and the lower belly.*

*6. Nails. Finger-nails and toe-nails.The nails were often associated with tied ribbons that matched other ribbons worn by the owner or maker. These dolls were habitually laid flat on their backs and seldom encountered standing up, so much so that the backs were often planed flat.*

*7. Separated scissor blades.*

*8. Human fingernails stuck into a wooden plank.*

*9. An assortment of separated genitals made in wood. There was a doll to be viewed essentially from behind and not from the front. The legs were squeezed closed from the front. The figure to be totally seen as though the figure was running away but could not conceal its sex. This figure also had wheels painted on its ankles.*

## CATEGORY 70. SMALL WHEELS.

*1. A wheel that could spin on a thin metal axle that looked through usage as if it would not last long before snapping.*

*2.A wheel pinned into a hollowed cavity in the chest, the axle protruding out through the arms at shoulder height on either side.*

*3.A collection of wheeled horse-spurs.*

*4.Small wheels. A single metal wheel, maybe from a clock, crudely thrust between the legs and fixed. The wheel could not be turned around. The genitals in the way of the wheel were only visible from the back, stuck between the buttocks.*

## CATEGORY 71. HUMAN SURVIVAL.

**It was discovered that many of the dolls of the Wouverain Mountains were either crippled or had no legs for some other reason, or that their legs had been amputated to make them shorter to fit into the available go-carts or coffins. It was a characteristic of the savage Continental Wars.**

*1. A white painted doll, turned on a lathe to resemble an oversized white chess pawn. It had a thumb fashioned from the fruit of the bean-tree soaked in vinegar to harden.*

*2. A headless doll turned on a lathe. Possiter Snacker took it to bed and laid it on her pillow in her house in the woods. When it was stolen on Bird-Fall Day, she was distraught and she went into hiding in the Trentamoir Forest. Her brother volunteered to make her another doll and she was lured out of the forest and rehabilitated. She still went to the forest edge and wept.*

[142] *3. A whittled holly-wood figure, eighteen inches high, leaving the bark unremoved on the torso to make a short textured jerkin, the protuberant belly and protuberant buttocks being painted white.*

*4. A dwarf doll wrapped in bandages, with a pacifier in its mouth.*

*5. A dwarf doll with false eyelashes made of short black painted wires.*

*6. A dwarf doll with a spine so curved its nose and toes almost touched.*

*7. Twin dwarf dolls joined at shoulder and hip. They were wrapped in laurel leaves. Laurel must never be set on fire because flames make it crackle loudly. Dendra Follit made the dolls a woven carriage, gave the carriage wheels, put the carriage in a paper bag and slung the bag around her shoulders and was never parted from it.*

*8. A dwarf doll wrapped in swaddling and lying in a cradle made of tree bark and lined with goose feathers. She made two pairs of stilts, one for herself and one for the doll, and the two of them walked the roads as a pair, leaving characteristic footprints of their passing. Four square ends in the mud.*

*9 A doll wearing a pair of spectacles without glass. She threaded the spectacles on a string and hung them around her neck. She never removed them, not even taking them off when her foster-mother bathed her.*

*10. A doll with two ancient copper-coloured coins for eyes. The coins had been battered with a stone until they had almost lost their markings. However, two stars and the letters RO were still just visible.*

## CATEGORY 72. SMALL WHEELS WITH ADDED LIGHTING

*1. A doll with a chest cavity filled with stinking offal wrapped in bandages along with a nail. It was said that the nail was present to attract a flash of lightning. "The lightning flash might just possibly bring the doll back to life." The doll's diminutive owner, Luxy Smattering, said that she would very much like that to happen. Luxy Smattering took the nail from the box every hour to moisten it on her tongue. "A moist nail was more likely to attract an electric flash than a dry nail. Maybe a nail moistened under my armpit might be even a better way to attract a lightning strike."*

## CATEGORY 73. COMING TO LIFE AGAIN.

*1. A small doll with a chest cavity lined in sheet tin that housed a dead snake which appeared to have perished in captivity.*

## CATEGORY 74. WISHING TO COME TO LIFE AGAIN AGAIN

**Small children often punished their dolls savagely, banging their heads on the ground and on tree trunks. They sometimes believed that punishment stired a doll into life. Then overcome with remorse, they copiously wept when the dolls fell apart.**

*1. A doll with cherry pips for eyes. The doll had a hollowed chest cavity.*

*2. A blue-painted doll with a square-sectioned chest cavity filled with various varieties of rotting flesh. The smell was too intimidating for close examination, but Izek made a drawing*

*that was signed by the three boys to signify their satisfaction with the drawing's authenticity to the original. Amongst the small rotting bodies, they noted a cat-fish, a king-fisher, a stoat, a crab-apple, a section of a wasp hive, a sheep's spleen, a cat's liver, a fungus in the approximate shape of a heart, a paper packet of ants, a pot of glue, the paw of a badger, a clutch of hibernating snails (these might have simply sought refuge in the doll, for the item appeared to have been abandoned and was hanging above an open drain) a dried-out-toad and a rat.*
*The dead bodies, as far as could be observed, were articulated with moveable heads, arms and legs pinned at neck, shoulders and hips. Then onto this vulnerability was nailed, stuck and pinned all manner of foreign objects, most of them from the South.*

## CATEGORY 75. FASCINATION FOR THE HUMAN FIGURE

**Toys associated with initiation, sometimes made from rabbits skinned to look like newborn babies.**

*1. Dolls impregnated with pepper. Some said to make the mother cough and sneeze to forget her pain.*

*2. Dolls soaked in vinegar. The bitterness and the sourness made the mother vomit to distraction.*

*3. Dolls covered in soot to make a black child. A black child was a coveted mystery.*

*4. Dolls covered in flour to make a white child. Such an event explains itself.*

*5. Dolls painted blue to make a blue child. A blue-blooded child was deemed desirable, reeking of regality.*

*6. Dolls painted red with a beeswax paint. A mystery here. Was it because the bees hummed you to sleep? Stung you into oblivion? Were industrious beyond belief.*

**Loadstar Fives who had brown hair and was aged forty-two wanted to become pregnant. Perhaps, relatve to this desire, she allocated special reserves from the funding to investigate pregnant dolls in the Thunder Mountains to the North of the Wouverain Mountain Range. She isolated rooms for the use of dolls. She started with preparing Room Eight which was to be associated with pregnancy.**

CATEGORY 76. SUCCOUR THE FUTURE.

**Descriptions of pregnant dolls. Seven different ways of making dolls look pregnant.**

*1. With a pouch full of eggshells.*

*2. With a bolster full of acorns.*

*3. With a pillow-case of hazel-nuts.*

*4. A small wooden doll had a drawer full of artificial flowers for a stomach.*

*5. A doll with masculine anatomy that had a compartment to hold a baby, though the baby was missing.*

*6. A painted doll with twins, one under each arm. It became fashionable.-*

*7. A doll with an intimated space for a womb, but in the small of the back.*

[146] **The ginger-haired Eerio Padebourne came down from the Wouverain Mountains to pay a visit to his old orphanage and to the Book Depository Building Offices. It was rumoured that the forty-two year old brown-haired Loadstar Fives was thinking to seduce the thirteen year old, ginger-headed Eerio Padebourne to give her a child. It was suggested that she wanted to have a child who was about to secure some sort of fame or notoriety by making an exhibition of toys, which largely might feature a propensity of toys that were dolls, replicas indeed of the human being.**

**This rumour was almost malignantly put into circulation by Opsinger Dedestry. Opsinger Dedestry suggested that Eerio Padebourne apparently used his supposed experiences with Izek Bable as a way to understand what was required of him. Eerie Padebourne grew to imagine that the success of the toy project required Loadstar Fives to become pregnant, though not by him. Opsinger Dedestry joked that Eerio Padebourne had become Loadstar Fives's toy-boy.**

CATEGORY 77. HUMAN SURVIVAL.

## Censored dolls.

*1. A wooden doll with the breasts removed, apparently with a saw.*

*2. A metal and wood doll with scratched out nipples.*

*3. A metal and wood doll without a mouth.*

*4. A doll without a navel. She could never have been born.*

*5. A doll where the eyes and the mouth had been plugged with a resinous gum found in old pine trees.*

*6. A doll with its arms fastened very firmly with iron nails over its breasts.*

*7.A male doll with missing eyes. Saucer Smith said that all males are blind.*

*8. A doll that hovered between being male and being female and deciding in the end of being of neither sex.*

*9. A doll whose ears had been bandaged tightly to its head and whose anus had been crammed with plaster, the supposition being that it could neither hear nor defecate.*

Lutumariner was becoming aware that a focus for the toy project could be concentrating on the search for dolls as toys on three accounts. First, on his own personal account, although un-detailed and under-stated, there were instructions to search for evidence of a matriarchal cult of life-size seated dolls associated with wheels. Two, it was apparent that the human form was especially present in toy representation and should be accommodated. Three, Loadstar Fives' desire to search for pregnant dolls was transparently related to her own desires to become pregnant.

Since the well-publicized demise of his wife, Opsinger Dedestry's interest in women had become reset. He had an interest in the Matriarchy of the Wouverain Mountains. A doll with all the right attributes could be a temporary substitute to redirect his lechery. He was prone now to take his own investigations in the Wouverain Moutains and it was soon reported that he was conspiring to abuse vulnerable members of the Wouverain Matriachies.

The three boys who had created the toy project scarcely comprehended these ambitions, but they were now it seems, corresponding with Izek Bable, the missing pastry-cook who had turned up with a pseudonym in Casteltrekar in the Oraleto Hills to the far North of the Wouverain Mountains, where the

[148] rainfall was uncommonly high. He, it seemed, encouraged the boys' enthusiasm to continue the research into toys, not restricting their attention at all to dolls, but embracing every aspect of their original ideas. He accused Opsinger Dedestry of the calumnies against him and he was certain that the success of the promised exhibition of the toys and its catalogue would help vindicate him and all those concerned. To earn a living, it was reputed that he had opened a bakery, specializing in mushroom-favoured pastries. It was obviously a provocation.

## CATEGORY 78. RESURRECTED.

**Dolls that had been buried and then exhumed. Families with children fleeing from intruders, assailants and plunderers had buried family treasures, children's toys amongst them, in cellars, outhouses, barns, privies, tree-houses, stables and wells. Agents eager to assist the three boys, Eerio Padebourne, Irium Botero and Jendro Hisloper, revealed them again to the open air.**

*1. A wood and cloth doll that patches of mold had made vulnerable.*

*2. A small doll that had lain for a long time in wet sand that, over time, had coloured its limbs an orange-yellow. The head and feet had resisted the colouring and had remained a dull matt black. Was this just an accident or was something indicated by this colouring?*

*3. A very large wooden and terracotta painted doll, more than three feet in height, found in wet clay. The arms had once been fixed at right angles to the body with rivets which had since rusted. The large doll could have been the same size as its child owner. Its body was covered in painted red kisses, evidence perhaps of a desperate departure.*

*4. A wooden doll that had been found next to the skeleton of a small female child, both buried in shallow leaf litter. Child and doll were holding hands.*

*5. A clay doll that had been buried with the intention of later exhuming it in the vain hope of being able to possess its skeleton.*

## CATEGORY 79. THE ULTIMATE COMPOSITE

**Composite dolls reconstituted from older models.**

*1. A rag doll with a removable wooden face.*

*2. A wooden doll with a plaster death-mask face.*

*3. A wax doll with a chewed paper face.*

*4. A limestone doll which had a head taken from a marble statue that had been eroded from a long stay in a fast-moving stream.*

*5. The wooden head of a man on a woman's body.*

*6. A wooden nose on a plaster face that had been replaced with a green nose made of green glass.*

*7. A wooden doll taken out of a tree. The doll had a visual sympathy with the tree.*

*8. A metal doll with a delicate porcelain face and delicate porcelain hands clenched tightly together as though in prayer.*

## CATEGORY 80. A PEOPLED WORLD.

**Toys that appear to have been fashioned to better see certain aspects of the world.**

*1. A toy with a piece of glass on a stick for looking around corners.*

*2. A toy with a sliver of glass on a stick for dazzling people at a great distance, maybe even from a distance of a mile.*

*3. A toy with two mirrors in a cylindrical box for looking over walls.*

*4. Two mirrors glued together to see yourself twice, once in full face and once in profile.*

*5. A polished metal cone fixed to a candlestick to increase the strength of the candle-light. There was a name, Ceramica, scratched on its shoulder-blades.*

## CATEGORY 81. ASSISTING MORE RESURRECTIONS

*6. A piece of bone, perhaps from the scapular of a large animal, that had been sanded so fine you could almost see through it. It was worn by children when looking directly at the sun at the time of an eclipse.*

*7. A blue enamel basin reserved for filling with clean water to catch the reflection of the full moon at night so that you might make a wish to meet your favourite person. A favourite person for girls under five was their absent mother. For girls over eleven their favourite person was their imaginary future husband.*

*8. Fragments of mirror jumbled in a box to be squinted at to imagine you were looking at the stars by day.*

*9. A handbag of broken mirror fragments kept as a treasure, because to throw a mirror away was always considered bad luck.*

## CATEGORY 82. THE BOX UNDERSTOOD AS A COFFIN

**Toy dolls associated with containers often still held their original contents in the form of oil, perfume, alcohol, even blood, even urine, as some sort of indication of revolt or opposition to orthodoxy. Thus the doll was an object of perceived apostasy or revolutionary activity. The apparent innocence of a child's toy, a doll, was often therefore an opportunity to make a container that might perform an iconoclastic function.**

*1. A simple plain wooden doll holding a box containing a human caul. The box was strapped to the belly of the doll. "If the baby's father is a sailor, give him the caul for him to take to the sea. To please a mother and make her feel comfortable, it will forever prevent the sailor from drowning."*

*2. A red painted box held in the left hand of a terracotta doll dressed as a soldier. The box held six musket balls that bore the marks of having been fired from an antique gun.*

*3. A wooden yellow-painted box containing dead ants.*

*4. A tin box with rusty hinges and a lid decorated with yellow flowers. It contained rusty pins, once presumably used in dress-making. The pins could have been temporarily held in the mouth of a seamstress. Maybe they had become rusty there.*

*5. A cheaply made wooden undecorated box containing broken walnut shells.*

*6. Stolen ribbons tied in bows and stored neatly in rows.*

*7. Hair, perhaps human, and likely to be of a child.*

*8. Twists of paper tied with cotton. These could be kite tails.*

*9. A dull and clumsy-looking doll with a large letter E printed on a square of parchment attached to the back of its neck. Testelrey said, "E is for elegant, eye, elsewhere, everlasting, evening, epilepsy, eventually, and 'nowhere' backwards."*

*10. A box without a lid full of earth and the skeleton of a bird and the remnants of a nest.*

*11. A box inside a box containing locks and keys.*

*12. A doll-shaped box showing evidence of dried spittle. It was contentious whether or not the spittle was human.*

*13. A small silver bucket that had apparently been associated with the sheath of a dagger.*

**Opsinger Dedestry sent a letter to Lutumariner to insist on a search for more life-like dolls. Lutumariner was irritated by Dedestry's presumption into interfering, but he did not check him. A pursuit to find dolls more true to life afterall was Lutumariner's objective as well.**

## CATEGORY 83. HUMAN SURVIVAL

**The three boys, Eerio Padebourne, Irium Botero and Jendro Hisloper went up to the Wouverain Mountains to investigate more fully the nature of the colonization of the mountains by the Wouverain female Matriarchy.**
**Some thirty dolls found and selected for their "illusion of reality". Here are descriptions of just six.**

*1. A doll with a pink clay face that had a leering expression.*

*2. A doll with a female head facing to the front and a male head facing to the rear. The faces were fashioned with expressions that respectively implied female humour and male pain. The intention without a doubt was to infer an ancient deity looking to the Future and the Past at the same time. Was the Future regarded as a male preserve and the Past exclusively to be considered as a female concern?*

*3. A painted wooden figure with metal pieces inserted for the eyes and the mouth. It had been found in a rubbish dump constructed by hemp-harvesters. The metal pieces had been fashioned in the South and were exceedingly well made and very lifelike, complete with eyelashes and the indication of a high-light in the pupil. When the metal pieces were removed from the doll, the exposed wood revealed heavy ravages caused by wevils.*

*4. A head and torso, both pierced with holes that bore marks of rust. The torso was far more realistically carved than the head.*

*5. A wooden figure with arms outspread and nail marks along the inner flesh of the arm ending with hands bristling with iron nails. Some eight nails were still embedded.*

*6. A figure with a hole bored right through the head from ear to ear and threaded with a string perhaps for easy carrying.*

## CATEGORY 84. REPRODUCTIVE RIGHTS.

## Excess sexuality in dolls.

*1. A pair of interconnected wooden dolls, the male unclothed and the female clothed, posed in an act of some amatory suggestibility.*

*2. An androgynous wooden doll, twelve inches high with removable body parts that could be attached to the wooden body by means of a heart-shaped metal pin.*

[154] *3. A doll with a delicate carved wooden detachable left ivory hand pointing downwards.*

*4. A doll with a left hand holding an object now missing. We could speculate on the missing item or items. Perhaps a cup. Perhaps even reins. Perhaps even a whip?*

*5. A doll of ambiguous provenance with two hands cupped in such a way as to hold a liquid, maybe once used as a drinking vessel but now ineffectual for three holes had been bored into the hands, perhaps deliberately to assist drainage.*

## CATEGORY 85. PREGNANCY ENVISAGED

**Esquila Fontenay was becoming a virago intent on revenge for passed misogynies and she was determined to seek justice. Lutumariner persisted in persuading her to desist in her punishment of Opsinger Dedestry. He failed, and abashed, he retired, even if temporarily, severely disappointed. His aims and ambitions were for the creation of a pacific new world in strict contrast to the recent troubles.**
**He had promulgated and established the great historical project of one hundred volumes. He had contributed to the Book on Conceptions. He had edited his Book on Births and he had started on his Books of Languages and Child Sicknesses and the volume on Names. He had made copious notes on other relevant subjects associated with a child's early life, but, feeling inadequate to start examining adolescence, he now began to feel a time had arrived to bow out, to retire from public life.**
**He was revered and honoured as the instigator of the Grand Scheme of the Hundred Books of the New Century. Esquilia Fontenay became his likely heir. Eerio was eager to depart to find the supposed location of the sea. Hisloper wrote the political history of the events surrounding the Toy Project. Esquilia Fontenay became the Wouverain Matriarch**

**exhibiting herself on her go-cart throne. Her image was bold and majestic. So Lutumariner essentially retired, and living with his wife in his tower-house in PastonCumber, his researches became private and remained unpublished. It was rumoured that he packed them up in fifty suitcases. He made a list of eight thousand dolls. All shapes and sizes, pigmies to giants. Wax and iron and papier mache. Some made to last. Some made to last only for a week. Here are only six of these thousand dolls on his list.**

*1. A wooden painted figure with a belt of detachable smaller females presumed to be children, all with mouths shaped in a pouting manner that suggested they might be whistling.*

*2. A naked female figure with a detachable wooden beard.*

*3. A black-stained wooden figure with a felt hat and a protuberant navel tied around with a cord.*

*4. A figure with detachable parts suggesting possible conversions from boy to girl. The wooden jointing on a tongue-and-grove carpentary principle was very fine.*

*5. A figure with detachable breasts that were hollow and filled with poppy seeds.*

*6. A plump, white-painted wooden female figure some five feet high with a hollowed-out space for a womb, the interior of which was lined with a red velvet cloth held in place with steel pins and brass tacks. Although the womb-space was empty there was a golden cord knotted at one end which could be presumed to be a representative umbilicus. This cord could be pulled through a vagina-like aperture between the legs. We might say that the evidence of midwifery was present.*

**Loadstar Fives was satisfied. Because she had found the toy of her childhood dreams. It was imprisoned in a swolln belly.**

[156] **After living six months with Eedio Padebourne, she announced that she was pregnant. It would seem that Eedio Padebourne was probably not the father. It was suggested that Opsinger Dedestry was the father. Loadstar Fives left a diary entry which implied molestation by an academic with the initials OD. No punitive action had apparently been taken, suggesting Loadstar Fives might have used the occasion of the molestation to deliberately become pregnant. Once pregnant, she took no further interest in the toy exhibition or its catalogue, though it was at one stage intended that an image of the five-foot-high white-painted wooden doll with a womb lined in red velvet was to be printed on the front cover of the first edition. Loadstar Fives retired, illegally taking fifteen per cent of the funding money. Nine months later she died in childbirth. The male child, Strepser Fives, survived. He was to become a Historian.**

**Whilst the Toy Collection consumed intense local interest in the Wouverain district East of PastonCumber, the Continent elsewhere experienced an eruption of a volcano, an outbreak of avian influenza among domestic chickens, an insurrection on the Eastern borders, a revolt of veteran soldiers felt cheated at the non-payment of wages for digging canals at Hellstand. There were floods at Geerly, poisonings in the regal households at Jostling, and intense poverty all over the North West due to drought and poor investments and a post-war feeling of apathy.**

**Such was Eerio's expansion of interest into other preoccupations, from about that time he began seriously to hand over the major responsibilities of the Toy Project to Jendro Hisloper, and he started to prepare himself for his determination to one day lead a definitive expedition to the South to find the elusive Sea. It was Esquila who showed Eerio the grave of her mother. He was recognised as Lutumariner's grandchild. And it would be twenty-seven years later before he lost his legs just like his mother had lost her legs, travelling too fast in a Racing Cart.**

# DEAD ANIMALS AS TOYS

## CATEGORY 86. REANIMATING THE DEAD

**Dead animals collected by Eerio Padebourne and Irium Bostero, and believed by them to have been treated as toys by orphan children.**

**The move to the promotion of the doll as a central image of the toy collection was gathering speed and significance. And this phenomenon was having an effect, as it were, of splintering sideways into various considerations like indeed of the possibility indeed of non-human animals possessing toys. A fact that many people had repeatably observed. It was recognised that intense friendships had occurred between totally unrelated animals, for example, of large monkeys for small dogs, wild horses for lost sheep, even for supposedly improbable relationships of carnivorous animals for herbivores, predatory fish fascinated by mollusks that could change colour, pedigree dogs for feral cats, mammals for birds and water-loving reptiles for fish.**

*1. An albino bird taken up by a black Sauris monkey fascinated by its startling white plumage.*

*2. A second monkey bleached a bird with quicklime solution to make it whiter and whiter till he poisoned it and it died.*

*3. A boy called Arcti kept a dead dog. He would not part with it though it stank and was covered with flies and maggots. He sat with it on his lap and talked to it, pulling its decayed tail until the tail came away and the boy, trying to fix it back on, burst into heart-rending tears.*

[158] CATEGORY 87. THE DEAD FANTASISED

*Recreated dead animals. Made-up dead animals and false animals reconstructed from various animal parts.*

*1. A rabbit with an eel for a tongue.*

*2. A monkey with wings.*

*3. A rat with a fish's tail.*

CATEGORY 88. KEEPING THE DEAD ALIVE

**Sleeping, unconscious and comatose animals kept by children as toys.**

*1. A goat drugged with hemlock.*

*2. A sheep paralyzed with the juice of holly berries.*

*3. A cat in a coma.*

*4. A naked cat shaved whilst made drunk with beer.*

*5. A weary frog which lost the capacity to hibernate and was carried around tucked up under a boy's hat.*

**There are painted images of a racing stallion called Elipse sharing a field with a goat nicknamed Francis, and a marmoset adopting a parrot, both of them foraging for seeds and soft fruit to please the other.**

CATEGORY 89. LIVE ANIMALS AS DOLL SUBSTITUTES.

*1. A pale green parrot with a bell around its neck.*

*2. A leech in a bottle fed on his brother's blood.*

*3. A black rat tied by its tail to a salt lick.*

*4. A slow-worm stuck in a wedding-ring.*

*5. A stag beetle fed on wild strawberries.*

*6. A hedgehog whose prickles had been painted red. It smelt and its faeces were riddled with worms.*

*7. A tortoise without a shell.*

*8. Various fish tied together by their tails that lived in a kettle.*

*9. A sparrow on a cord fed with fly grubs.*

*10. A goldfinch on a silver chain sat on a perch on the wall. It had been famously painted.*

*11. A sheep with a cleft pallet.*

*12. A lamb with a docked tail and pierced ears.*

*13. A ram with painted horns.*

*14. A ram with artificially sculptured horns.*

*15. A marmoset with extracted teeth and a wooden collar.*

*16. A cat with a paw permanently jammed in a scent bottle.*

*17. A stag with a doll's house tied between its antlers.*

**Led by Eedio Padebourne the matriarchy sought out Opsinger Dedestry and by a trick and a deception that involved practically no violence, handed him over to the women of the Wouverain Mountain who were keen to have him pay for pimping their daughters. The women of the Wouverain Mountains imprisoned Opsinger Dedestry as they knew best. Lutumarine was alarmed. Without a doubt, knowing that**

[160] **Opsinger Dedestry was guilty of multiple crimes including intimidation, financial embezzlement, blackmail, sexual harassment, and possibly rape and murder, Lutumariner nevertheless was convinced that Dedestry's summary imprisonment and the revenge potential of the Wouverain Mountain Female Community to cancel his presence in the PastonCumber Environment, was inimical to society at large which was seeking peace, and reconciliation and due process of law. And certainly the success of the Toys Project was in great danger of adverse publicity. He sought to adjudicate and summoned the toy project's administrators to discuss his anxieties. Little was resolved. Sections of the Wouverain Matriarchy were determied to admonish Opsinger Dedestry.**

**Jendro Hisloper and Irium Bostero in joint charge, took over the exhibition preparations. The doll collection had been a profound education for them. They knew how to continue to finish this exhibition, give exhibitions publicity, and prepared them as adults to manoeuvre people to their advantage. This is true of their future exhibitions on Bird Feather Management, the Custodianship of the Sea Explorers and the Far North Policy towards the eradication of the ice. Their thesis now was that all toys lead towards human metamorphosis and that the exhibition should be structured on that premise.**

CATEGORY 90. ANIMALS WHO KEPT THEIR OWN TOYS.

*1. A monkey with a puppy. Perhaps the canine was the result of a conjunction of spaniel and greyhound. The monkey, a Bald Capuchin, fed the dog on wet bread and slugs.*

*2. A dull gull which was infatuated with the spendid appearance of a bird of paradise.*

*3. A dog with a dogfish kept in a shallow puddle. If the puddle would have been deeper, the two animals would never have been able to rub noses.*

*4. A pig with a human baby. The hungry pig had pulled the baby from its cot. The baby had chewed ears and toes. Knowing no other parent, it kept close to its surrogate mother, was suckled by it and hugged it for comfort and survival. The baby had learnt to grunt and puddle in the mud.*

*5. Two sows who shared a baby-girl and fed it sorrel and peelings, and quarrelled over which should eat her faeces.*

**In the course of their research, the child Historians and their minders had discovered three things. One. That the pursuit, manufacture and ownership of toys is a microcosm of human life in general. Two. That children are savage animals surviving through guile, force, bullying and chicanery in a hostile world. Three. That interference with natural laws produces long-term disaster and great human misery.**

**It had been observed publically even by Opsinger Dedestry that the ultimate toy was always another human being.**

## PEOPLE AS TOYS

### CATEGORY 91. GIRLS KEPT AS TOYS.

*1. Bibikilouse had red hair and a birthmark on her belly suggesting a fighting cockerel whose feathers fringed her navel like a dancing skirt. She was to be represented in the catalogue and the exhibition, if there was to be one, by drawings by Fester Primes.*

*2. Marike's second child Pinkyory, who, always expecting pain, screamed when touched, even by dogs and birds. She was to be*

[162] *represented in the catalogue and the exhibition, if there was to be one, by drawings by Habitoris.*

*3. Pollidory Hippo had black eyelashes but mousey hair and big feet. She always took off her shoes in company. She was to be represented in the catalogue and the exhibition, if there was to be one, by drawings by Sizerea.*

*4. Jersie Optima had eczema in her armpits. She was afraid of white horses and vowed that they were responsible for her affliction.*

*5. A girl aged eleven who was mute. She put her right index finger to her lips asking everyone to observe silence in her presence.*

*6. A girl aged eleven who could cook eggs but had a trick of dribbling blood from her nose to scare away predators.*

*7. Georing Figura who had thick fingers.*

*8. Magna Pistoris who had slit eyes and had arrived from the South wearing a plum-coloured dress.*

*9. She had a mouth made red and swollen with too much fingering.*

*10. Who had pierced ears.*

## CATEGORY 92. FEMALE TRANSFORMATIONS

*1. There was a girl with a tail. She was prized and claimed by several policemen who came to blows over her that ended in blindness for one of them. They drunkenly made up and blinded the girl with a stick as a compensating act.*

*2. A girl who scratched her palms raw and kept her hands gloved "wrapt in hand-shoes" manufactured of inside-out rabbit fur by her best friend Salivera who came from the South via the Sideways Mountains.*

*3. Twins who had identical birth-marks on their buttocks. Some say artificially branded there by the heated end of a lensless spy-glass that had famously been used to look out for the Sea.*

*4. A girl who had iron in her soles. Literally.*

*5. A girl who had a tuning fork buried in her spine. It could still be twanged to E flat.*

*6. A girl called Tressa who constantly trembled, having suffered badly in an earthquake, never permitting anything on or over her head because of being buried alive in dirt and glass fragments for six days. She always slept in the open air and hysterically avoided cracks in the earth. She was attached to a copper-miner called Strachey who was her sole protector and who painted his name on her forehead to prove it. He kept her chained to his bed when he worked at the mine all day. His obsession was to protect her whatever happened. He treated her like a queen.*

*7. A girl who had charred combs permanently fixed in her burnt hair.*

## CATEGORY 93. BOYS KEPT AS TOYS.

*1. Took out their milk-teeth to give to toothless pensioners. It was reasoned that the boys would lose their milk teeth soon enough and here was an opportunity to re-use them.*

*2. Tried to make them female. He failed.*

*3. Made them fat.*

*4. Made them race on the backs of turkeys.*

*5. Taught them to swim to catch crayfish off the shallow river Gissing Beach*

## CATEGORY 94. WOMEN KEPT AS TOYS.

*1. Scooter had been imprisoned in the Cocerary Flats as a milk-machine.*

*2. Censored.*

*3. Censored.*

*4. Censored.*

## CATEGORY 95. MEN KEPT AS TOYS.

*1. Captured soldiers called Sebastians were imprisoned at Jeffrey Stones Marketplace in Baintry. They were forced to wear borrowed uniforms from which the medals and insignia had been removed. Two coloured targets were painted on their chest armour which had been made by children. They had been painted green and purple, the colours of the Mirage, with embossed crimson hearts spiraling in on golden nipples manufactured with bottle tops. The Sebastians, sometimes called Mantegnas, were used for target practice, and later their wounded bodies, with the arrows extracted, were locked up at Goetery Edge. The soldiers had perished because of their injuries. "Wooden armour is no protection against metal projectiles." They were buried at Sedgebastion Tor. Their wooden armour, product of a child's imagination and ingenuity, is to be exhibited.*

*2. Censored. A young male with ten circles painted on his outer wooden casing-armour, was killed, and arrow marks were drilled deep into his wooden armour.*

*3. Censored. A young wooden man with air holes punctured into his palms and his feet.*

*4. Censored.*

*5. Censored.*

**Discovery was made in the Upper Wouverain Mountains of the physical presence of rail-tracks as intimated in the copiously discovered maps of the same.**

# DOLLS ON WHEELS

CATEGORY 96. WAS THE MOST ANCIENT TOY A DOLL?

**Eerio Padebourne and Irium Bostero and Jendro Hisloper climbed the second highest peak in in the Wouverian Mountains called the Stringley Tor. And straight away they discovered the rails that wound and twisted round large boulders, disappeared into the dark of low-ceilinged tunnels and across ravines where water splashed far below. They came across side-rails, points and sidings where go-carts were abandoned, some rusting, some still decorated with fading mountain flowers. Some of the four-wheeled go-carts supported wooden chairs which contained seated wooden female dolls.**

**The women had engineered eight domains named after celebrated female icons of the distant past. And they had, over the years, built a system of rail tracks to unite the eight**

[166] domains complete with terminal junctions, multiple-points systems and sophisticated turntables. They had started their endeavour some thirty years before whilst escaping the atrocities of the South-North divide. To bolster their courage and confidence, they had organized festivities and competitions, riding the system of tracks across viaducts and through tunnels and along embankments with go-carts. These were primitive at first and then growing more complex and sophisticated, often becoming elaborate. They held annual and biannual races and soon found many occasions for monthly, even, in some cases, weekly occasions, to hold seasonal competitions with handicaps. Perpetua had become instrumental in their sophisticated organization. She has persuaded Lutumariner to assist her. They became friendly, had indeed fallen in love, and had children. And grandchildren. Then disaster struck. Perpetua crashed and smashed her legs, became a cripple, forced to be strapped into her elaborate go-cart, and pregnant with Esquila Fortenay. Lutumariner a fifty-year-old and retired artillery officer at that time, was distraught. She delivered the infant Fontenay. She died soon after, bleeding to death. They kept her blood. They built a replica of her, tailored-made from the size of her toes, to the colour of her hair to the shape of her fingernails.

The boys ventured further into the Mountains. Eventually it seemed every female had a representative doll. Usually self-made though invariably assisted by the activity of others.

Each woman sent their representatives to the races. Sometimes they raced themselves. A Commuity of virtuoso go-cart females developed.

Dolls have been manufactured for thousands of years. Ancient people had made dolls, and in every conceivable material possible, clay, wax, stone, marble, paste. There was much referencing of ancient dolls. Lutumariner said that the original toy had been a doll.

Dolls sitting on Go-carts

*1. The first example found was of a four-wheeled go-cart with the doll sitting facing forward. There was a unity between the doll and the car with its rear axle cut through the hips.*

*2. The second example found was much the same, but with the addition of a cat carved from wood sat on the belly of the female figure.*

*3. The third example found was not dissimilar to the other two but was covered in an animal fat that still seemed fresh.*

CATEGORY 97. PRIMACY OF THE FEMALE

## Dolls seated on rudimentary Go-carts

*1. Doll figures were sitting up with legs outstretched, the wheels now placed at seated hips and ankles.*

*2. The same with a stake protruding from the middle of the back maybe to push and steer the cart.*

*3. The seated wheeled females were now provided with a regular platform to sit on.*

*4. The same with a detachable figure and some elaborate decoration on the cart.*

*5. Of wings made of slats of wood.*

*6. With feathered wings.*

**There was an isolated seated female figure in a go-cart with large red spoked wheels. She had her eyes closed and her head was slightly tilted backwards. Was she posed in some sort of ecstasy? She was dressed in a white frock. It was said that the**

[168] garment could not be clothed in anything else. It was considered that the correct word was indeed, a frock. A frock, not a dress or a robe, but a frock, a simple garment as worn by a child. A grown-up child. A child wishing to be grown up. She had breasts and a pronounced belly. It might be perceived that the figure was pregnant. She had plump arms and a small mouth. There could almost have been breath coming from that small mouth as though it was cold winter's evening. Her feet were naked. She wore no shoes. There was a frill of some sort bordering the lower hem of the frock. The go-cart had been parked there probably for some time, probably for more than a short time because there were grasses growing under its crude pneumatic tyres. Perhaps indeed the doll indeed had been sitting there for a month, even perhaps three months. Maybe even nine months.

They fetched Lutumariner. At first he did not want to come. He examined all the dolls and he wept.

## CATEGORY 98. PALATIAL GO-CARTS.

Emboldened by his research, freed from the embraces and attentions of Loadstone Fives, Eedio Padebourne went searching for toys in the Northernmost parts of the Lower Wouverain Mountains where, seeking independence, the Wouverain Matriarches had deeply settled, seeking independence. On a recent estimate there were some sixty to a hundred thousand women female members of the larger community, with some eight thousand subsidiary settlements of various social structures . The women could claim a deep history going back two hundred years, but the recent Troubles had swelled the original numbers, providing a sanctuary for the dispossessed female, humiliated in bad marriages, in sexually exploited communities, war widows, females with no original means to be financially secure. They had evolved a democratic series of communities, differing in political severity from the most radical to communities of prostitutes living off dispossessed soldiers, maimed prisoners of war, deserters and reprobates, idealists and people of indeterminate sex.

Eedio Padebourne announced what he was looking for and in a mule stable near Moltantine he was taken to what can be described as a Wouverain Harvest Festival Facility. Elderly matriarchs, as carpenters and waggoners, created harvest carts on wheels primarily to bring in the rye and oats harvest ceremonially, choosing a Wouverain Maid to represent the autumn fertility. Prime among the exhibits was a palatial cart on wheels. Basically a pine-wood box on four eighteen-inch circumference wheels with a steerage foreplank supported by two smaller four-inch circumference wheels. All the wheels were made of yew-wood painted with red lacquer, and then tyred in plaited rope copiously soaked in beeswax. Leather steerage ropes were tied to the front axle. The sitting box, capable of accommodating three people, was lined in a dark red cloth, there were footrests, a padded seat and padded armrests and a wooden brake with a handle fashioned from an umbrella with a yellow duck's head. The carriage or go-cart was built around the Wouverain Maid's Chair. The carriage had not been used for three seasons and needed some reconstruction, refurbishment and the collecting and refinement of parts dissembled and hidden in various households.

*1. A pair of leather horse-riding boots with bucket-tops had been nailed to the steerage bar. They were stuffed full of crumpled paper for warmth, and tied around with crimson ribbons for gaiety.*

*2. Attention had been made for the comfort of the driver with a padded bucket-seat with marked depressions for the buttocks.*

*3. Trailing ribbons and smoke.*

*4. Turning knives on the back-wheel like some ancient mythical queen who had been infamously flogged with her daughters.*

[170] *5. A celebrated old box go-cart that had run many flights hung up on a bedroom wall complete with a fabric doll stuffed with sawdust. The doll was naked with newly painted pink buttons for nipples.*

*6. With wings made of pine branches*

*7. With wings made of feathers*

## CATEGORY 99. PERPETUA.

*1. A large articulated female doll was finally found. She was seated in an iron frame chair on wheels that ran on a narrow gauge railway track across the Wouverain Mountains. Her name was Perpetua. The name was written across her breasts. The ultimate doll had been definitively discovered for the Wouverain Mountains.*

*2. The life-size doll was made of five chopped-straw-filled bolsters, for torso, upper limbs and lower limbs. With the upper limbs and lower limbs tied with twine to articulate the hinges of elbows and knees. The doll was fitted with accessories made of wood, being the head, two white-painted breasts with pink-painted nipples, wooden hands and feet with articulated fingers and thumbs and toes. The head was made of oak with blue glass eyes, a deeply sculptured mouth with a removable tongue and front teeth, removable ears and nose, and a full wig of ginger human hair made such as to be removable on the principle of a scalp. When the wig with its section of wooden scalp was removed the top side of the brain had been carved into the solid oak. Damage included some wood-worm, peeling white paint on the breasts, some rust marks on the upper limb bolsters, some evidence of dormice nesting in the torso at the lower back.*

*3. When the exhibition opened, this doll was exhibited in the atrium. After six months, it was returned to Lutumariner's library and a facsimile was made and placed at the very end of the exhibition, right by the exit.*

Lutumariner's search had been rewarded. He was shown the life-size doll dressed in a white frock from the waist down, seated in the wheeled chair that could run on rails. He was persuaded to recognise it as an effigy of Perpetua, the one-time matriarchial leader of the Wouverain Mountain female community.

He was grateful that the effigy had been found and made a statement that he had been an enforced stud thirty-four years before in the Wouverain Mountains where he had always believed he had fathered at least twenty children, all, it was said, possessing ginger hair. The doll called Perpetua was her representative likeness. And Lutumariner acknowledged that Eedio Padebourne was his probable grand-son. He used his powers as a Chief Historian to have the doll confiscated and set it up finally in his library of thirty-three thousand books in the Northern part of the city of PastonCumber. Because of a perceived conflict of interest, he withdrew his active support from the toy project, though he did not in any way stop or interrupt the finances. He created a personal finance foundation for the continued education and well-being of his titular grandson, Eedio Padebourne, rewarded the Orphanage for their care of the named orphans, promised an investigation of the activities of Opsinger Dedestry relevant to the engrossment of his responsibilities and set in motion a rehabilitation programme for the restitution of the reputation of Izek Bable, falsely accused of irregularities.

It was generally agreed that if Lutumariner ever admitted to owning and treasuring a toy, this Perpetua was that toy, a resplendent doll seated in a cart on wheels always ready for a chariot race in the Wouverain Mountains.

It was presented as the introductory item of the exhibition. And the recovered Jill-in-a-Box toy was presented as the very last toy in the exhibition, permanently set to deliver its optimistic message.

[172] CATEGORY 100. THE HUMAN BODY AS A TOY.

**The community of females abused by Opsinger Dedestry took a revenge on the body of their exploiter and torturer. They snatched him from his prison and commenced their activity by turning him into a collection of toys, planning to demonstrate his last day alive with drawings and diagrams. Lutumariner had lost. Esquila Fontenay had won. She had her revenge.**

*1. Pulling out his hair, making a wig.*

*2. Stuffing his mouth with earth and stones.*

*3. Pulling at his fingers till the knuckles cracked.*

*4. Wrapping sticky bandages with a tenderness around his limbs only to rip them off again with a great violence.*

*5. Demanding that he should bleed to make their care for him more realistic, cutting open his belly and pouring in red ink, opening up his navel, creating an umbilical opening that they might fill it with a false umbilicus made of twisted rope smeared in butter. They played at difficult births, wrapping the false umbilicus around his neck until they had half-throttled him.*

*6. They thrashed his buttocks till they were crisscrossed with five-laned scratches.*

*7. Buttons were sewn to his nipples with coarse thread.*

*8. They twisted his genitals around and around in a torque till he screeched with alarm and pain and wept and vomited with the humiliation.*

**Opsinger Dedestry died with a sharp forked stick forced up his rectum.**

**A tattoo was written on his perineum to indicate his crimes. It was sliced from its position in a skin section three inches by half an inch and fixed in a glass frame.**

**The women planned to exhibit Opsinger Dedestry's remains in a small white-painted cupboard, much like his cupboard beside his bed in the Wouverain orphanage.**

*1. The girls severed Dedestry's head and used it as a football, playing the game with bare feet until the head became such a mess of hanging tongue, gouged eyes and ripped ears, they wrapped it in a wet sack and continued to bounce it about the slopes and inclines of the mountains from summit to summit, until the jaw came loose and it no longer rolled very well.*

*2. The limbs were severed and hung on a cross-bar to make a swing.*

*3. The trunk was stuck with threaded needles and made a scarecrow to scare away the starving crows from pecking at the February cabbages.*

**The stink of the corpse in its severed parts persuaded Esquila Fontenay and her associates to bury the head, the torso, the hands and the upper legs. The rest of Opsinger Dedestry's body had disappeared. After burial for nine months, for as long as Opsinger Dedestry had been in his mother's womb, the impatient girls dug up his skeleton.**

## OPSINGER DEDESTRY AS A TOY

**Opsinger Dedestry's bones as toys are displayed in the cupboard beside his bed in the orphanage, lit by artificial light that minimises shadows.**

*1. Knuckle bones from a left hand dipped in mulberry dye in the act of playing Fives.*

*2. A femur for a bat bound at one end with binding twine to make a handle.*

*3. The pelvis polished to make a toy-dog basket.*

*4. The brain pan for a bowl to contain wooden marbles.*

*5. Teeth to be drilled to make a doll's necklace.*

*6. A finger bone as a teething ring.*

*7. A marrow-hollowed tibia to make a three-note flute.*

*8. A scapula to throw against the wind to return it to its sender.*

**The intended exhibition of exactly ten thousand toys arranged in one hundred categories in twenty-five rooms, was finally prepared by the boys Eedio Padebourne, Irium Bostero and Jendro Hisloper and their minder, Izek Bable over two floors of the PastonCumber Book Depository Building.**

**The catalogue of toys is still being prepared. It is largely based on this present text as regards the toy descriptions, including indications where censorship has been seen to be necessary. The final definitive catalogue publication will omit the anecdotal information of orphanage politics, post-war bureaucracy, gossip and History included here in bold type in order to make the catalogue educationally useful and relevant for public consumption. It will concentrate exclusively on the lists of toys.**

**The catalogue that accompanies the exhibition certainly demonstrates the imagination and resilience of children under stress, their strength and ability to, in essence, as always, make something out of nothing, or something out of very little indeed, is very heartening. We take it as an example for civilization to continue in great hope - post the recent troubles - and be an optimistic and prophetic indication of the much-awaited coming renaissance.**

*THE END*

www.disvoir.com
www.facebook.com/groups/disvoir/
www.instagram.com/dis_voir_edition_production

EAN 978-2-38162-008-4

PRINTED IN EUROPE

Printed with help of

Région îledeFrance